Heartland™

Amy's Journal

Lauren Brooke

SCHOLASTIC

Read all the books about Heartland:

www.scholastic.co.uk/zone

To Linda Chapman.
Without her, Heartland's story would never have been told...
With love and thanks

With special thanks to Linda Chapman

Scholastic Children's Books,
Euston House, 24 Eversholt Street,
London NW1 1DB, UK
A division of Scholastic Ltd
London ~ New York ~ Toronto ~ Sydney ~ Auckland
Mexico City ~ New Delhi ~ Hong Kong

First published in France by Pocket Junior, an imprint of Univers Poche, 2003
This edition published in the UK by Scholastic Ltd, 2006

10 digit ISBN 0 439 95582 3
13 digit ISBN 978 043 995582 9

Printed by Nørhaven Paperback A/S, Denmark

10 9 8 7 6 5 4 3 2 1

A Letter from Amy

Hi!

Most of you probably know all about me and my home, but for those of you who don't, my name is Amy Fleming and I live on a farm called Heartland just outside Meadowville in North Virginia. My mom started Heartland twelve years ago when I was four. It's an equine sanctuary. We have eighteen stalls and we take in horses and ponies who are physically and emotionally damaged. Using alternative therapies, we rehabilitate these damaged horses and find them new homes. We also take in boarders with behavioural problems. Their owners pay for us to cure them and this money helps support the rescue side of things.

My mom started Heartland after she and my dad split up. They were both showjumpers but then Dad was in a riding accident that left him unable to ride professionally again and their marriage broke up under the strain. Mom returned to Virginia — she'd been living in England with Dad — and a year later she started Heartland. She built it up from nothing and it became really successfull, but then just over a year ago, Mom was killed in a road accident. Since then I've been running Heartland with my grandfather, my older sister, Lou, and Heartland's stable-hands, Ty and Ben. Grandpa looks after the house and the land — the farm belongs to him. Lou, who is twenty-three, runs the business side of things and Ty, Ben and I look after the horses. Ben's been working at Heartland for a year — he loves to showjump and has a gorgeous jumper called Red. Ty has been working at Heartland for four years now — at first he used to just help out at weekends and in the vacations but two years ago he left high school and started working with Mom full-time. Ty's brilliant with horses — he's also my boyfriend and he's very cute!

Anyway, like I said, at Heartland we use lots of alternative therapies. Mom was an expert on horse behaviour. She believed that most horses who misbehave only do so because they are scared or in pain. She taught me that instead of beating a horse up for misbehaving, you should try and work out what is causing the problem. Nine times out of ten you'll sort the behaviour out — and in doing so you'll end up with a much better relationship with your horse. In this book I thought I'd share some of the things that have happened in my life with you and some of the other things Mom taught me too. If you want to read more, look at my list of favourite non-fiction books. All the books I put on that list are written by really inspirational people, and although they write about different things and different training techniques, they all have one thing in common — they all want to make the world a better place for horses. And that, as far as I'm concerned, is the most important thing of all.

Happy reading!

Amy

PS At Heartland we use alternative therapies to complement conventional veterinary medicine. If your horse is ill or starts acting strangely the first thing you should <u>always</u> do is call your vet.

Chapter One

How I Discovered Join-Up

One of the most important training techniques that we use at Heartland is a method called Join-Up. Mom learned about it from an inspirational horseman called Monty Roberts. I remember when I first saw her join-up with a horse. I was ten years old and I had never seen anything like it in all my life. . .

Mom led the appaloosa filly into the circular ring. I shut the gate, the metal warm beneath my fingers. It was only nine o'clock in the morning but already the sun was heating up. It was going to be another long, hot summer day. I watched as Sasha, the three-year-old filly, looked around, her head high, her eyes flickering uncertainly. She had spent most of her life running free with a group of other youngsters, but now her owners had sent her to Mom to be broken in – or "started" as Mom preferred to call it.

I leaned against the gate. "What do you do first?" I asked.

The night before, she had got back from spending a few days visiting a horseman called Monty Roberts. He had shown her a training method he had developed called join-up. It was a way of getting a horse to trust you, and he used it to start young horses as well as to help horses with problem behaviour. Mom was going to try it with Sasha and she had said I could watch and help.

"Well, first I set her free," Mom told me.

"You set her free?" I said in surprise.

I had watched Mom start plenty of horses before, and it had never involved taking the halter off and letting the horse loose. Usually Mom would work the horse on a long line until it was relaxed around her and then she would slowly introduce the bridle and then a saddle. It always took a long time to start a horse – Mom might spend up to six weeks working with a horse before she actually tried to ride it. She said that it didn't matter how long she had to wait, having the horse trust her was far more important than starting it while it was still afraid – if you didn't have that, she always said, you didn't have anything.

Taking off the halter and long line, Mom stepped away from the filly. Sasha looked surprised. Putting her head down, she sniffed at the sand and started to wander away. Mom tossed one end of the long line towards the filly's chestnut-and-white flecked hindquarters and raised her arms. With a slight jump of surprise Sasha trotted away to the side of the pen.

"What are you doing?" I asked.

"I'm using my body language to communicate with her," Mom told me. "Just as if I was a horse in a herd."

She moved to the centre of the ring and, fixing her eyes on Sasha's, she pitched the long-line at the filly's quarters again. With a snort, Sasha broke into a high-headed canter. Keeping her cantering round, Mom started to explain to me what she was doing.

"Horses use their bodies to communicate with each other all the time," she said. "When an older mare tries to discipline a younger horse she chases it away from the herd. She keeps it away by using an aggressive body posture. When the younger horse shows that it's prepared to be submissive and wants to be friends then the mare lets it back into the herd. That's what I'm going to do. Watch. . ."

Keeping her eyes fixed on Sasha's, Mom raised her arms again. The appaloosa cantered on. When she had gone six times round the pen, Mom moved her body slightly to the front of her. Sasha stopped with a snort. Mom took a step towards her and she set off in the opposite direction.

After the filly had completed five circuits in the new direction, Mom spoke. "Look, Amy," she said quickly. "Watch her inside ear."

Sasha's left ear had flopped over slightly. It was pointing into the circle in Mom's direction. "That shows she's ready to start listening to me," Mom told me. "It's her way of telling me she wants to stop cantering round."

"So are you going to let her stop?" I asked.

"Not just yet," Mom said, pitching the rope at the filly again. "She's got to give me some stronger signals first."

After a minute or so, Sasha's head started to tilt towards the inside of the circle. Slowing to a trot, she started to make chewing motions with her mouth, almost as if she had a mouthful of grass.

"What's she doing?" I called in surprise.

"That's her way of signalling that she respects me and that she wants to be friends. All I need now is for her to lower her muzzle to the floor." As Mom spoke, Sasha stretched out her head and neck so that she was trotting along with her nose almost touching the sand. "That's it," Mom said, sounding suddenly excited. "OK, this is where the join-up part comes in."

Mom turned her shoulders sideways on to Sasha and looked at the floor. Sasha slowed to a walk and then to a halt. She looked at Mom's back with a slightly puzzled expression. What was going to happen next?

Giving a soft snort, Sasha started to walk towards Mom. She walked all the way to the centre of the ring, stopping only when her muzzle touched Mom's shoulder.

Mom turned slowly and rubbed her forehead. "Good girl," she murmured. I was about to ask what was going on but before I could, Mom suddenly started walking away from Sasha. To my surprise, Sasha followed her.

First Mom circled to the right and then to the left. Sasha

walked behind her, following her like a dog. I stared. Wherever Mom went, Sasha did too. It was like there was an invisible rope binding them together. I had never seen anything like it.

At last Mom stopped and rubbed Sasha between the eyes again. Then she turned to me. Her eyes were shining.

"Did you see the way she was following me?"

I nodded. "Why was she doing it?"

"It means that she's realized I'm not a threat. By following, she's showing me that she trusts me and accepts me as her leader. Now we've got that understanding, she will be much easier to handle and start." Mom started to pat Sasha all over. The filly stood completely still, letting Mom touch her everywhere – on her back, her hindquarters, her stomach. Her eyes looked soft and relaxed and never left Mom for a second.

"Let's try her with the tack," Mom said, slipping thelong-line on to Sasha's halter at last. "Can you bring everything over?"

I took the saddle, saddle pad, extra long-line and bridle off the top of the gate and carried them into the ring.

"Put it all on the floor so Sasha can have a look at it," Mom told me. "And then go back to the gate just in case she panics or I need to send her away again."

I did as she asked. Climbing back over the gate I saw that Sasha was sniffing at the tack. When she had lost interest in it, Mom lifted the saddle cloth and placed it on her back. Sasha stayed quite calm, so Mom picked up the saddle. Holding it on her right hip she moved quietly to Sasha's side and gently lifted it on to the filly's flecked back. Sasha's ears flickered uneasily.

"It's OK, girl," Mom murmured, rubbing her neck. Sasha relaxed.

Mom moved round to the far side of her and lowered down the girth. Moving back to the left side, she smoothly brought the girth into place.

I tensed. No matter how slowly you started a young horse, most of them hated the feeling of having a girth fastened around their middle. Mom always said that the pressure on their back and tummy made them think they were being attacked. I waited for Sasha to freak but she just stood there. Mom quietly buckled up the girth and then unclipped the long-line and moved away, standing well out of reach of Sasha's back hooves.

"Off you go," she said, clicking her tongue. Sasha took a step forward and then, feeling the saddle as she moved, hunched her back in alarm. Mom adopted an aggressive body posture. Squaring her shoulders on to Sasha, she pitched the long-line at her again. Sasha set off at a canter, bucking three times as she went. But then to my surprise, she stopped bucking and settled down to cantering round the ring. After a few minutes Mom blocked her and sent her round the other way. After three circuits Sasha had lowered her head and neck and was chewing with her mouth just as she had done before. Turning her shoulders on to her, Mom invited her to come and join-up again.

Sasha stopped and walked quickly over to Mom's shoulder. Praising her, Mom rubbed her face. Then she picked the bridle off the floor and slipped the bit into Sasha's mouth. Sasha grabbed at the metal but stood still while Mom did the buckles up. When the bridle was fastened up, Mom glanced round at me. "You can go and get your hat and body protector now," she said.

I stared at her. My hat and body protector? What did I need them for?

"That's if you want to ride her of course," Mom said, with a slight smile.

"Ride her?" I exclaimed, staring. "But you've only just put the saddle on for the first time!" Usually Mom spent at least a week after first doing that before trying to sit on the horse's back.

"I know," Mom told me. "But that's the beauty of join-up. Because you've communicated with the horse in a language it understands, you've got its trust and so it'll let you ride straightaway." She smiled at my astonished face. "Now go and get your things and we'll see."

I raced down to the tackroom. When I got back Mom had attached the spare long-line to Sasha's bit and was long-reining her in a circle. I put on my hat and fastened up my body protector as Mom asked Sasha to trot and canter in both directions. Finally she stopped her and asked her to rein back one step.

Sasha did as she asked and Mom stroked her. "OK," she called, looking round. "She's ready for you now."

I walked across the pen, not knowing whether to feel excited or nervous. For a year now, Mom had been getting me to help her when she backed ponies and the smaller horses. I loved it, but you never quite knew what a horse would do the first time it felt someone on its back. I wondered what Sasha would be like – after all she had only just had a saddle and bridle put on her for the first time.

"Say hello to her by rubbing her forehead," Mom said,

unfastening the long reins. "It's more of a non-threatening gesture than patting her."

I did as Mom said. Sasha lowered her head and snuffed at my hands with her chestnut nostrils.

Mom tightened the girth and clipped one of the long reins on to the near-side bit ring. "We'll do just the same as normal," she explained. "First I want you to lean over the saddle – we'll see if she's happy with that."

I moved round to Sasha's side and Mom legged me up so that I was lying on my stomach over the saddle. I stroked Sasha's shoulder. She was standing quite steadily.

"I'll walk her round a bit," Mom said.

She didn't even need to pull on the long-line. As soon as she set off, Sasha followed her trustingly. Her strides swung me from side to side. It wasn't very comfortable but Sasha seemed quite calm.

"Great," Mom said, stopping her after a few circles. She took hold of my left foot and guided it gently into the stirrup iron. "Now you can try sitting astride. But remember, sit up very slowly."

I nodded. Stroking Sasha's neck, I eased my right leg over the saddle so I was lying flat against her neck, and then as Mom rubbed her face, I slowly sat up. Sometimes when a horse sees a rider sitting up on their back for the first time its instincts take over and it panics, thinking the rider's a predator who has landed on its back, but Sasha stayed quite still, her nose touching Mom's chest.

I sat there in the sun stroking her neck and playing with her wispy chestnut mane. "Isn't she being good?" I said in astonishment.

"Very," Mom smiled. "Shall we try a walk?"

I nodded.

Clicking her tongue, Mom led Sasha around the pen. The filly didn't even tense up. Seeming to accept that everything Mom did was OK, she walked quite calmly, her ears pricked.

"That will do for today," Mom said, halting her in the centre after she had circled twice in both directions.

I dismounted and glanced at my watch. It was just ten o'clock, only an hour since Mom first brought Sasha into the ring, and now she had not only accepted the saddle and bridle but she had been ridden for the first time. I looked at Mom in wonder. "She was brilliant!"

"Join-up makes starting a horse so easy," Mom said. "It shows it that you speak the same language, that you'll listen to it and that it can trust you. You allow the horse to select you as its leader instead of forcing it to accept you."

"It's amazing!" I said.

Mom smiled at me. "And everything you do together after that is a partnership."

Chapter Two

How I learned to Read Horses' Faces

At Heartland we believe that you can tell a horse's personality by looking at his face. The shape of his eyes, muzzle, nostrils and ears can all tell you something about his temperament. I remember the day my mom first taught me about reading horses' faces. It was few days after my twelfth birthday. We were at Bull Ridge Farm — a local livery stable. Mom had been called there to work with a gelding called Ziggy who hated to load. After an hour's work of joining-up with him, Mom had him walking happily in and out of his owner's trailer.

Clicking her tongue, Mom walked towards the ramp. Ziggy followed her, his chestnut ears pricked. Without the slightest hesitation, he walked into the trailer. Mom halted him inside. "Can you put the ramp up for a few moments, please?" she asked softly.

I hurried forward and helped Mrs Rosen, Ziggy's owner, heave the metal ramp up. As we shut it I could see Mom patting Ziggy. His ears were flickering slightly but he looked quite calm.

"That's great!" Mom called after ten seconds. "You can put it down again now."

We lowered the ramp.

"It's amazing!" Mrs Rosen said, as Mom backed Ziggy out. "Last time I tried to load him it took me three hours! You've worked a miracle, Mrs Fleming."

Mom rubbed Ziggy's forehead. "Not a miracle. I just showed him he could trust me. You should have no problem with him from now on if you work with him like I did."

"Thank you so much," Mrs Rosen said, taking Ziggy's lead-rope.

I patted him.

"We should get going," Mom said.

"What about payment?" Mrs Rosen asked her.

"Oh, I'll send you the bill at some point," Mom said. I had a feeling this would probably lie around in our kitchen at home for ages. Mom just hated dealing with paperwork.

"Bye," I said to Mrs Rosen, and, after giving Ziggy a last stroke I followed Mom towards the car. I loved going with her when she went to visit horses with their problems. People thought she was amazing. Around our area everyone called her "the horse lady".

"That was cool," I said as we headed towards the car park. "Mrs Rosen seemed really pleased."

Mom's blue eyes lit up as she smiled. "Yes. Hopefully she and Ziggy will now be able to get on with their life together without fighting every time she wants to put him in a trailer. . ." She broke off, frowning

I followed the direction of her gaze. To one side, there was a trail leading up into the hills. A dark bay horse was standing on it, his tail swishing, his ears back. Even from a distance I could see that his rider, a girl who looked about nineteen, was trying to urge him on but he wasn't moving. She smacked him with her whip. He threw his head up and stepped back. She smacked him again. Getting increasingly agitated the horse moved sideways and backwards, but he wouldn't go forward. As she smacked him for the third time he half-reared.

"I think she needs some help," Mom said quickly.

Quickening her pace, she hurried towards the trail. I jogged after her.

By the time we reached them, the horse was throwing his head up and backing up fast. "Walk on, Aztec, you dumb animal!" the girl shouted, kicking him hard.

"Can I help?"

Hearing Mom's voice, the girl looked round. "This jerk of a horse won't go forward," she exclaimed. "Will you chase him from behind for me?"

"No," Mom said.

The girl stared in astonishment. "Pardon me?"

"I'm sorry, but I don't think that's the best way," Mom said, her voice calm but firm. "There must be a reason your horse is behaving the way he is. If you don't find out what and deal with it, then you'll just have this problem time after time." The girl looked angry, but before she could say anything Mom stepped forward, holding out her hand. "Marion Fleming," she said pleasantly. "From Heartland."

A frown of recognition crossed the girl's face. "Oh . . . the horse lady?"

Mom smiled. "That's what some people call me." She motioned to me. "This is my daughter, Amy."

"I'm Christina," the girl said, introducing herself. "I've heard about Heartland," she said, looking interested, "that's the place for abused horses, isn't it?"

"We like to think of it as somewhere to help horses in trouble," Mom corrected her. "So what's the matter with your horse?"

"Oh, him!" the girl said disparagingly. "He's got a real attitude problem – he's as stubborn as they come. Every time I try to ride him away from the barn he starts to baulk like this. The only way I can get him to go on is if someone chases him from behind." She shook her head. "I only bought him a few weeks ago. He seemed OK when I tried him out, but he's turned out to be really difficult. Buying him was a big mistake. I reckon he's just one of those problem horses."

I glanced at Mom. I had often heard her say there are no such things as problem horses, just owners who have a problem understanding why their horses act like they do.

"I see," was all Mom said now. "So, what are you going to do with him?"

"Sell him, I guess," Christina said with a shrug. She sighed. "It's a pity, though. He's not bad in the stable. In fact, he's really affectionate. It's just when he's out that he acts so dumb."

"Maybe he's scared, in pain or unhappy," Mom said quietly.

Christina looked at her. "What?"

Mom stroked the gelding's cheek. "You're not just out to be awkward, are you, Aztec? You're not a mean horse." She looked at his rider. "That's clear from his face."

I wondered what she meant. Christina seemed just as bemused. "What?"

"If you get off for a moment," Mom said, "I'll show you what I mean."

Christina hesitated for a moment but then meeting Mom's steady blue gaze, she did as she was asked.

Standing beside me, she watched as my mom traced the fingers of her right hand along Aztec's nose. "People used to say that a horse's face will tell you what his personality's like," she said. "There's an old saying, 'good eye: good horse'. I've always found that to be true. And it's not just the eye that you should look at. The shape of the horse's face, the ears, the nose – they all give you clues. See Aztec's straight flat nose? A profile like that is usually found on a horse who's uncomplicated and steady. He's got large and round eyes, which suggests he's cooperative and affectionate. His nostrils are large and delicate, usually a sign of intelligence. And finally his ears." Mom's fingers moved to Aztec's ears. The gelding lowered his head and she massaged the base of them gently. "Look how wide apart they're set. Horses with ears like that are usually reliable with a good capacity for learning." Mom glanced at Christina. "Everything about Aztec's face suggests that he should be a wonderful horse to own and ride – steady, dependable, quick to learn and cooperative."

Christina frowned. "That's really weird – that's almost exactly how his old owner described him."

"But not how you've found him to be?" Mom said.

"No, although. . ." Christina looked thoughtful. "I suppose he is like that in the stable, and he's been fine the few times I've ridden him in the ring. It's just been whenever I've taken him out on the trails that he's played up."

Mom stroked Aztec's neck. "I think he's been trying to tell you something. His face shows he's not the sort of horse to be difficult out of sheer cussedness. It's my bet that there's something wrong and he's been trying to communicate it to you."

"What sort of thing?" Christina asked, looking interested.

Mom smiled. "If we figure that out, we could solve his problem." She threw a questioning look at Christina. "That's if you want to, of course."

"Yes, yes I do," Christina said eagerly. Her earlier defensiveness had vanished. "Do you really think you can help me?"

"I'll try," Mom said. "So," she looked around. "Is it just this trail he plays up on, or is he the same going out on all the trails?"

"There's only one other trail," Christina replied. "I haven't used it because it leads out on to the roads."

"Well, let's try taking him along it," Mom said. "If he's truly afraid of being out, he should play up when you try to ride him out in that direction too. If he isn't then," she looked around at the trail we were on, "we try and find out what it is about this trail that's causing him such a problem."

Christina remounted and Mom and I walked beside Aztec as she rode him back down the trail. The second trail led out of the yard behind the barns. Aztec set off along it quite happily, his ears pricked, his stride swinging out.

After five minutes, Mom said, "Well, he clearly seems happy going along this trail."

"So it must just be the other trail that's upsetting him," I said.

Christina halted. "But why should it? It just leads past some fields into the woods. There's nothing there to frighten him."

"From a human point of view, maybe," Mom said. "But we need to look at it from a horse's. Let's go back and take another look."

Christina turned Aztec round and returned to the first trail. As soon as Aztec stepped on to it, his ears went back and his head lifted. He stopped, his body tense.

I looked around. The trail went uphill, winding round a corner. On either side of the trail were fields filled with horses and ponies. There didn't seem to be anything that might scare a horse.

"What is there round the corner?" Mom asked Christina.

"Just some fields that have been empty for a few months," Christina said, looking puzzled. "Then the trail goes into the woods."

Mom looked at Aztec. "Maybe I'll just take a quick walk up there. You stay here with him, Christina."

I followed Mom.

"Something's got to be upsetting him, Amy," she said, as we walked to the corner. "Look out for anything, no matter how small. A loose sack, an old oil drum, a piece of farm machinery –

anything like that could be spooking him."

I scanned the fields but there was absolutely nothing. Like Christina had said, round the corner there were just empty fields. The grass was churned up into mud and scattered across the fields a distance away were a number of corrugated metal pigsties. The smell of the pigs still lingered very slightly on the air. "I can't find anything that might upset him," I said turning to Mom.

Mom was looking at the churned-up field. "Pigs," she said slowly, speaking half to herself. "These fields have had pigs in them. That could be it."

"What do you mean?" I asked.

"Maybe Aztec's scared of pigs," Mom replied. "Many horses are."

"But there aren't any pigs here," I said in surprise.

"But Aztec doesn't know that," Mom said and turning, she hurried back down the trail.

I ran after her. I didn't know what she meant. "I don't get it," I called out.

"Put yourself in Aztec's position," Mom said. "He's coming away from the yard towards a corner. He doesn't know what's round the corner but he can smell pigs. If he's scared of pigs, what will he do?"

"Stop," I said. "Refuse to go on."

Mom flashed a smile at me. "Exactly."

We reached Christina. "Did you find anything?" she asked quickly.

"Did Aztec's last owner say anything to you about him not liking pigs?" Mom asked.

Christina looked puzzled. "No, she didn't."

"I've got a hunch I know what's wrong with him," Mom told her. "But I need to find out if he's scared of pigs. Have you got his owner's telephone number?"

"Yes, it's in my mobile," Christina said.

"It might be a good idea if we gave her a ring," Mom said.

I held Aztec while Christina found her mobile and made the call to Aztec's previous owner. Finally she pressed the off button on her phone.

"You were right," she said, looking astonished. "Aztec is scared of pigs. His owner said she forgot to mention it – apparently he's never liked them. He was bred on a small-holding and when he was a foal he got too close to a sow and her piglets and she chased him." Christine frowned. "But what's this got to do with the way he acts on the trail? There aren't any pigs in the fields at the moment."

"But he can't see round the corner, and his sense of smell is telling him that there are pigs there," Mum said.

"So that's why he's stopping?" Christina said.

Mom nodded. "I'm sure of it."

Christina looked amazed. "So he's not just being lazy and stubborn."

"No, he's scared," Mom said.

Aztec snorted. Christina walked forward and stroked him. "I'm sorry, boy. I didn't realize." She looked remorseful. "To think I thought you were just being naughty."

Mom stepped forward and patted Aztec. "At least, now you know why he's behaving like he is, you can start working with him to help him overcome his fear."

"Will you help me?" Christina asked her.

Mom nodded. "It may take some time to cure him though," she warned. "His fear is going to be pretty deep-rooted if it goes back to when he was a foal. You'll have to be prepared to be patient."

Christina nodded. "I don't care. I just feel so bad about the way I was treating him. I just didn't know. I didn't understand."

Mom looked at her sympathetically. "It's OK. The important thing is that you're prepared to help him now. You're not the first person to have misunderstood a horse – and you certainly won't be the last."

"So, how can I start working with him?" Christina said eagerly.

"Well, first of all," Mom answered, "you need to start by joining-up with him. . ."

Two hours later, Mom and I finally got ready to leave Bull Ridge Farm. Mom had shown Christina how to join-up with Aztec, explaining to her how it would help them rebuild their relationship.

"When he trusts you, you'll be in a position to help him overcome his fear," Mom said as Christina followed us to the car. "What you need to do now is show him that you can be depended upon. That will come through join-up."

Christina nodded. "I really liked doing that join-up stuff."

Mom smiled at her. "Good." She opened the car door. "I'll come back tomorrow and we'll work some more then."

"Bye," I said to Christina as I got into the car.

Mom started the engine and we pulled out of the parking lot. Christina waved.

"It's like she's a different person," I said, remembering the way Christina had been smacking Aztec with her whip when we had first seen her just a few hours ago.

"Like a lot of horsy people, she's just never been taught that it's possible to have a relationship with a horse based on trust and respect instead of domination," Mom said. "Hopefully, today I've started to show her that there is another way – that she can have a far more fulfilling relationship with her horse if she's prepared to listen to him, trust him and accept he has his own point of view."

I thought about the way Mom had read Aztec's face. "I liked the way you looked at Aztec and knew what his personality was."

Mom smiled. "It's good to be able to read horses' faces. Particularly horses who are behaving badly. If you get a horse like that who doesn't look mean or stubborn then you can be pretty sure that you should be looking for another reason for his behaviour. It helps you understand horses. It's just a case of recognizing that horses, like people, are individuals with their own personality traits."

I was fascinated. "So what do you look at?"

"You look at the horse's profile, at the shape of their ears, eyes, muzzle, nostrils. You look from the front and from the side. It all adds up to give you an impression of what the horse's personality is like."

"Will you teach me how to do it?" I asked.

Mom nodded. "Yes," she promised. "I will."

Over the next few weeks, Mom visited Christina and Aztec regularly. I went with her and watched as the horse started to trust

Christina more and more. A month after we had first seen him, he was following Christina around the yard with no lead-rope on and soon he would even follow her up the trail. Whenever he hesitated, she accepted that he was trying to tell her he was unhappy, and she would take him back down to the yard where she would work him in the ring for five minutes before trying again. Because she listened to him, his confidence and trust in her grew and within two weeks, he was walking round the corner after her.

The first day she rode him up the trail, Mom and I watched together. Aztec walked happily up the trail with Christina talking softly to him. A minute later they disappeared around the corner and were lost from sight. Mom put an arm round my shoulders and hugged me. "I think we have a happy ending," she said softly.

Mom kept her promise about teaching me to read horses' faces and slowly over the next few months, she taught me all the things that she believed. Being able to read horses' faces has really helped me at Heartland. If I hadn't known how to do it I might have believed, along with everyone else, that horses like Promise and Feather were dangerous and should be put down. Instead their faces seemed to tell me that neither were mean by nature, and so I looked for other reasons for their behaviour. The next chapter shows you some of the horses from Heartland, and a description of what their faces show about them.

Chapter Three

Reading Horses' Faces

Pegasus

long straight profile – brave, bold, steady
bump above nose – demands to be treated with respect,
a dominant character
high-set, pointed eye – clever, self-confident
long mouth – fast learner
slanting muzzle – potentially stubborn
large, curved, wide-set ears – very intelligent, steady

Sundance

broad forehead and dished face – intelligent, loyal
bump above nose – demands to be treated with respect,
a dominant character
high-set, pointed eye – clever, self-confident
slanting muzzle and grooved chin – stubborn
curved, close-set ears – intelligent, unpredictable

Storm

slightly dished face – intelligent
large round eye – thoughtful, affectionate, willing
large open nostrils – bold, confident
blunt round muzzle – cooperative
curved, wide-set ears – very intelligent, steady

Red

straight profile – straightforward, uncomplicated
medium-sized eyes with large eyelid – average intelligence,
affectionate
long chin – slow learner, needs clear instructions
medium-sized ears set far apart – cooperative, willing

Promise

dish face with bump above nose – sensitive, self-confident,
needs to be treated with respect
almond-shaped eyes – affectionate, intelligent
large open nostrils – bold
delicate curved ears with tips that point towards each other –
high intelligence, empathy with rider

Feather

dish face — sensitive
low-set almond-shaped eyes — affectionate, intelligent,
potentially timid
small delicate muzzle — very sensitive
delicate curved ears with tips that point towards each other —
high intelligence, empathy with rider

Melody

low-set round eye – affectionate, willing, potentially timid
rounded small muzzle – gentle, cooperative
average size nostrils – average intelligence
rounded small ears – cooperative, needs clear instructions
or may panic

Daybreak

long profile – brave, bold
high-set, pointed eye – clever, self-confident
bump just below eyes – resistant, dominant
long mouth – fast learner
slanting muzzle and grooved chin – potentially stubborn
long straight ears – temperamental

Chapter Four

How I Found Sundance

"Nine hundred! Do I hear nine hundred?" the auctioneer's voice rang out above the noise of the crowd gathered in the sales barn. Standing around a circular pen, the onlookers watched as a pretty grey filly cantered around the pen, her head high.

A young woman standing near to me and Mom held up a card with a number on.

"That's nine hundred dollars to the lady in the green coat," the auctioneer said, nodding at the woman. "Do I hear any more?"

I looked at the grey filly. Her large dark eyes were fearful, her muscles were tense. I didn't like horse sales. The horses always looked so bewildered. I tried to imagine what it must be like for them, cantering around the noisy pen, not knowing why they were there or what was happening or who all these people were.

"Any more bids, ladies and gentlemen?" the auctioneer called. There was no response. He paused and then raised his hammer. "Going, going, gone!"

I glanced at the lady. She was smiling. I hoped that she would give the filly a good home.

"Next we have Lot 122," the auctioneer called as the pen gate was opened and the filly allowed out. An old bay hunter was next in the ring. He was skinny with a sway back, but he had a noble face and wise eye. He looked round in confusion and I felt awful. He looked like he should be grazing happily in a quiet field, and now who knew what would happen to him? A lot of the horses who came to a sale would end up being sold for meat. At the thought of the fate awaiting the bay in the ring, I felt suddenly sick.

"I need to get some fresh air," I said to Mom.

She nodded. "OK, I'll meet you by the trailer in half an hour."

I pushed my way through the crowd. The barn smelled of stale sweat and horse droppings. Reaching the entrance I walked outside and breathed in deep gulps of the damp March air. It was a relief to be outside, away from the scared horses and the shouting. Mom had come to the sales to see if there were any horses who needed Heartland's help. I just wanted to take them all home.

I looked around. Nearby was a barn with a cluster of metal pens. Each pen had a pony inside, waiting for their turn in the ring. The ponies were to be sold after the horses. Prospective buyers were now walking round the concrete walkways, examining the ponies and reading the notes attached to the pen gates.

I walked over. A brown-and-white paint pony was looking over the gate of the first pen. I stroked her nose and read her notes:

Lot 244: Scout. 13.2 h.h. mare. 15 years old. Has competed in equitation and hunter pony classes. 100% to load, shoe, clip and in traffic. Ideal first pony.

Scout nuzzled my hands and I fed her a horse-cookie from my pocket.

"She'd make you a lovely pony," a man standing nearby came over. "Are you looking to buy?"

"No. . . No, I'm not," I said, and hurriedly moved on.

There were so many ponies to look at. Old and young, all different shapes and sizes from a tiny black Shetland to a handsome bay hunter pony, whose card said it had won a string of prizes in the show-ring. As I walked towards the back of the barn, I saw a group of three men standing around a pen, their arms crossed.

"Unwarranted," I heard one of the men say, shaking his head.

I went closer. I couldn't see which pony they were discussing.

"Pity. He's a good-looking animal," the third man said, going closer to the pen gate. "And young too. Feed him up and you could get a good price for him."

There was a clatter of hooves. I saw a glimpse of a golden coat and heard a clang of metal as the pony threw himself at the pen gate. All three men jumped back.

"Vicious brute!" the first man shouted, waving his arms angrily. "Go on! Get back with you!"

The pony shot to the back of his pen. Shaking their heads, the men moved away and I saw the pony for the first time

He was beautiful, a buckskin with a dirty gold coat and a tangled black mane and tail. His head was high. His ribs stuck out and there were deep grooves in his quarters, but the look in his eyes was so full of pride and spirit that it seemed to make him glow with energy. He looked around, daring the world to come near him.

My eyes went to the card on his door. There was no name. Just the words:

Lot 247: 14.2 h.h. Gelding. 9 years old. Sold unwarranted.

I looked at the pony again. I felt drawn to him, to his fire, to his spirit.

"I wouldn't go too close to that pony, honey," a voice said behind me.

I swung round. One of the men who'd been by the buckskin's pen had seen me standing there and had come back.

"He's vicious," he told me. "He just tried to take a bite out of my friend." He shook his head. "The glue factory's the only place for a creature like him. You stay away from him or you'll get hurt." He nodded, walking off.

I hesitated and then looked back at the buckskin. He had tried to attack the men – I'd seen it. But was he really vicious? He looked so beautiful.

I scanned his face. His eyes were large and set high on his face. *Intelligent eyes. Proud eyes.* The words sprang into my mind and suddenly I remembered everything Mom had been teaching me about reading horses' faces. I could hear her voice in my head: "If a horse is behaving badly then look at his face. Do his features tell you he's mean and aggressive? If not then look for another reason for his behaviour – he may be in pain, he may be scared, he may simply be misunderstood."

I started to look more closely at the shape of the buckskin's features. His wide forehead signalled intelligence. His long narrow ears suggested he might be temperamental. He had large, defined nostrils – another sign of intelligence. And just above his nostrils, he had a bump. That, combined with his high-set proud eyes suggested he was a dominant horse who needed to be treated with respect. Everything about this nameless pony suggested he was intelligent and proud. He was stubborn, but not mean – certainly not vicious.

Just then a beam of sunlight flashed through a broken slat in the barn roof and danced on the pony's golden coat. His eyes flickered to mine. Suddenly I felt a charge rush through me, and I knew that I just had to persuade Mom to buy him.

"I'll be back," I told him and, turning, I ran down the aisle.

Mom was still beside the noisy ring. "Hi," she said, looking round as I pushed my way to her side. I was out of breath and she frowned. "What's up?"

"There's a pony!" the words burst out of me. "We've got to buy him, Mom! We've just got to!"

Mom looked surprised.

"Come and see him!" I begged. "Please!"

For a moment, Mom's eyes scanned mine and then to my relief, she nodded. "OK."

I turned and began to push my way out through the crowd. "Come on!"

Mom followed me.

As we got out of the auction barn, I started to tell her about the pony. "He's 14.2 hands, a buckskin. He's being sold as unwarranted. And has a vicious reputation, and likely that he'll go for meat. But he's not mean – not deep down. I know he's not."

"You read his face?" Mom said. It was half a question, half a statement.

I nodded. "You wait till you see him," I said, heading down the aisle that led to his pen. "You'll see what I mean."

The buckskin was still at the back of the barn, standing in his pen, his head raised.

I watched Mom's face as she scanned his head.

"Potentially stubborn," she said softly. "But very bright. Proud, brave, confident, complex – a pony who needs respect."

"That's what I thought!" I said in excitement. "It's his eyes and that bump on his nose."

The pony looked at us.

Mom read the card beside him. "So you heard some people say he's vicious?"

"I saw him try and bite them," I admitted.

"Why?" Mom asked curiously.

"One of the bidders went up to the gate," I replied. I looked at her beseechingly. "Can we buy him?"

"I'm not sure yet." Her eyes fixed on the pony, Mom stepped towards the gate. The pony's ears went back. Mom stopped and turned sideways on to him. She lowered her eyes. I knew what she was doing. By turning away from him and avoiding direct eye contact, she was trying to make herself seem as unaggressive as possible. By not walking up to the gate, she was respecting his space and waiting for him to make the first move. The minutes passed. Several people came by the pen, but when they saw that the card read "unwarranted" they walked away again. It was quiet near the back of the barn and no one took any notice of what Mom was doing – no one that is, apart from the pony. He watched her intently.

The first of the ponies to be auctioned was led out of the barn by a handler. Still Mom waited. Suddenly the buckskin snorted and brought his head down slightly. Mom took a small step away from him. He lowered his head even more and stared at her.

"That's it," she whispered. "Good pony."

He took a step towards her. There was nothing fearful about

him, although his eyes showed a wariness. Step by step he moved closer to the gate until he was close enough to put his head over. He snorted again and then reached out with his muzzle and touched her shoulder.

Mom stayed very still for a moment, and then raised her hand and stroked his nose.

"There," she whispered. "You're not bad, are you?"

Slowly she backed away. The pony watched her and in his eyes, I saw a glimmer of softness.

Mom looked at me. "Yes," she said. "We can bid for him. He may have his problems, but deep down I think we'll find a very good pony in there."

I was delighted. "Oh, Mom, that's great! You really think we can help him?"

"No, but I think *you* can," Mom said.

I looked at her, wondering what she meant.

"You found him, Amy," Mom went on "You saw something in him that made you look beyond his behaviour. If we buy him then you should be the one to work with him."

"Me?" I stammered. I'd helped Mom with the horses, but I'd never worked with one on my own before.

Mom nodded. "You're more than ready to work with a horse on your own now, and I think this pony could be a very good starting point. I'll help you of course, but he'll be your responsibility. You can plan out his care, his training, you can work with him each day – if you want to."

I looked at the beautiful buckskin in delight. It would be like having a pony of my own. "Want to?" I exclaimed. "I'd love to!"

"Good," Mom smiled. "We'd better get ready to start bidding then."

"And now on to Lot 247," the auctioneer called. "A nine-year-old buckskin gelding. Sold unwarranted." There was the sound of shouting and the metal gate of the round pen swung open. The next instant the buckskin cantered into the ring, urged on by two handlers. Seeing the people, the pony stopped dead and pinned his ears back.

One of the handlers headed towards him. "Go on!" the man growled, swinging a rope.

The buckskin stared at him proudly and then, snaking his head down, he charged at the handler. With a yell, the man vaulted over the gate. Stopping with a defiant squeal, the buckskin stamped a front hoof down, sending a spray of sand into the air. A murmur of surprise ran through the crowd

The auctioneer cleared his throat. "So, Lot 247," the auctioneer said. "As you can see, a spirited pony. . ."

"Vicious, more like!" someone called from the crowd.

The auctioneer ignored the call. "What am I bid?"

I looked round anxiously. If the price went too high we wouldn't be able to buy the pony and right at that moment I wanted him more than anything else in the world.

The pony shook his head and squealed again.

"Who will start the bidding at six hundred dollars," the auctioneer asked.

No one in the crowd moved. Pinning back his ears the buckskin charged at the front row of people. They drew back hurriedly as he thudded into the barrier.

"Five hundred?" the auctioneer said. "Four hundred and fifty."

His voice was sounding increasingly desperate.

I glanced at the little group of meat-men. For once even their hands were still. The pony was skinny and trouble.

"Come on, ladies and gentlemen," the auctioneer encouraged. "A nice-looking pony like this. What am I bid?"

"One hundred and fifty dollars," Mom said, her voice ringing out

There was a surprised murmur. Everyone turned to look in our direction.

"One hundred and fifty dollars!" the auctioneer exclaimed. "Any advance on one hundred and fifty dollars? Look at his head, ladies and gentlemen, there's breeding in that head – he'd make a nice little pony, just needs some work. You're not seriously expecting me to sell a pony like this for one hundred and fifty."

The pony charged again at the fence and the audience gasped.

Seeming to decide that enough was enough, the auctioneer hastily brought his hammer up. "Going to the lady in the blue jacket on my left. Going, going, gone," he said, the words rushing out of him as he banged the hammer down to close the sale. The clerk wrote down Mom's number and I hugged Mom in delight. The pony was mine!

It took four handlers to get the pony out of the ring and back into his pen. Mom went to the office and paid and we fetched a halter from the trailer. "I want you to try and get the halter on to him," Mom said as we walked to the pen. "Just do what I did before.

Stand and wait for him to make the first move."

"When do I put the halter on?" I asked.

"When you feel he's ready," Mom said.

The pony was standing at the back of the pen, his body tense. We stopped a couple of metres away from his gate. He stared at us and then snorted. It was as though he recognized us.

I walked forward and, hiding the halter in one hand, did just what Mom had done. Within ten minutes, the pony had come to the gate and was standing with his nose by my shoulder. "Here," Mom said, slipping a small tin into my free hand.

It was a tin of her special powder that she made from herbs and old bits of chestnut – the horny growths on the inside of horses' legs. I had seen her use it with new horses many times. It calmed them down.

Moving slowly so as not to alarm the pony, I eased the lid off the tin and rubbed a little of the gritty grey powder on to my hands, then I held out my palms towards the buckskin. He snuffed at them and then lifting his muzzle to my face, he breathed out. I breathed in his sweet hay-scented horsy breath and breathed out softly. He snorted and lowered his head.

I slowly lifted the halter and fastened it on to his head. All the time his dark eyes watched me but, to my relief, he accepted my touch. I unbolted the gate.

"We're going to take you home now," I said.

"Ask him to come with you, Amy, don't tell him," Mom said quickly. "He's got to feel you respect him. If he feels that, I'm sure he'll do what you want."

"Shall we go to the trailer?" I asked the pony.

He looked at me for a long moment with unblinking dark eyes and then he stepped forward and followed me out of the pen. As we walked up the aisle, I felt people looking at us and nudging each other. Clearly everyone was stunned by the change in him.

Smiling to myself I led the pony out of the barn and over to our trailer. Without hesitating, he followed me up the ramp and inside.

"Well done," Mom said, putting up the ramp and coming round to the jockey door. I looked round and seeing the pride in her eyes, I felt suddenly warm.

"So what are you going to call him?" she asked, as I got out of the trailer.

I thought for a moment and glanced back inside at the buckskin, who was now pulling at a haynet. Suddenly I remembered how, in the barn, the sun had streamed in through a gap in the roof and danced on his golden coat.

"Sundance," I replied.

Chapter Five

My First Show

It took me months to fully gain Sundance's trust, but by spending time with him every day, grooming him, massaging him, working him in-hand and eventually riding him, I eventually won through with him. It was worth it. As I started to ride him more and more it became clear that he was a brilliant natural jumper. Mom helped me to train him and then in the summer I took him in my first show. We entered the Large Pony Hunter class at a local hunter show at East Creek Farm.

"Just take it steady," Mom said, holding Sundance while I mounted.

Soraya Martin, my best friend, patted Sundance. "He looks gorgeous!" she said. She loved horses as much as I did and had been helping me get Sundance ready for his big day.

I gathered up my reins. Soraya and I had spent hours cleaning my tack the night before and it was gleaming. "Go and work-in away from the other ponies, Amy," Mom went on, straightening my stirrup leather and checking my girth. "When you think Sundance is relaxed, then come back here and Soraya and I will come to the warm-up ring with you."

I nodded and, patting Sundance's golden neck, I touched his side with my heels. He walked forward eagerly.

I rode him behind the trailers to where there was an empty field. There were people unloading horses and ponies, and grooms hurrying around with buckets full of brushes and tack. Over by the two show rings there were lots of very smart-looking horses and ponies. I noticed that they were nearly all bays, chestnuts and greys. Clearly those were the colours that judges in the hunter classes tended to like. I just hoped that the judge of my class would like buckskins too!

I stroked Sundance's neck. "We'll show them, won't we?"

Sundance snorted and, blocking thoughts of the other riders out of my mind, I asked him to trot. For fifteen minutes I circled him at walk, trot and canter, feeling him start to relax and come down on to the bit as Mom had taught me.

At last, I patted his neck and slowed him down to a walk. "Good boy," I told him. "Let's go and find Mom and Soraya and try a few practice fences."

Loosening my reins, I let him walk out on a long rein back towards the trailers. A girl came riding towards me. She was riding a beautiful dark bay pony with two white socks and a white star. With her navy-blue show jacket and long blonde plait she looked very smart. Suddenly I realized I knew her. It was Ashley Grant — she went to the same elementary school as me and Soraya. She was in a different class to us and we never really talked to her much at school but now I was just glad to see a familiar face. "Hi!" I called, waving.

Ashley's bay pony shied in alarm and Ashley only just managed to avoid falling off. Grabbing her reins and re-finding her lost stirrup, she glared at me. "What did you do that for?" she demanded angrily.

I felt my cheeks going red. "I'm sorry," I stammered. "I was just saying hi."

"You should be more careful!" Ashley snapped. "Otto's very highly-string. He's part-thoroughbred." She glanced at Sundance whose head and neck were stretched out lazily. "Though I can see you wouldn't understand about that. What's your horse's breeding?" She laughed scornfully. "Part mule?"

I looked at her angrily.

Ashley looked down her nose. "Whyever did you get a buckskin? Everyone knows they never win anything."

"Maybe I don't care about winning," I retorted.

Ashley snorted. "Just as well!" she called, riding off.

I stared after her furiously. How dare she talk about Sundance like that! I rode back to the trailer, feeling really mad.

"Your mom's just gone to take another look at the course," Soraya said, jumping off the ramp as I rode up. "She said we should meet her at the warm-up ring," She suddenly saw my face. "What's up?"

"That girl from school – Ashley Grant," I exclaimed. "I saw her just now on this pony – he was gorgeous but she was awful! She said Sundance was part mule and that buckskins never win!"

"She didn't!" Soraya said. "What an idiot. Sundance is beautiful. You've got to beat her now, Amy!"

I looked round to where Ashley Grant was working her pony in. "Just watch me try," I said.

I rode Sundance over to the warm-up ring, with Soraya walking beside me carrying the grooming kit. There were about twelve ponies in the ring, all going in different directions. Several trainers was standing in the centre, shouting at their riders. It looked very busy and I felt very glad when I saw Mom standing near the gate. She looked her usual calm self.

"How's Sundance?" she asked, coming over.

"OK," I said, deciding not to mention my meeting with Ashley Grant. "He was going well when I warmed him up."

"Great. There's about six more riders before you," Mom said. "So let's take him into the ring and pop him over a few jumps."

She walked into the ring and stood by one of the practice fences. I trotted round a few times and then cantered towards it. Sundance's ears pricked and he increased his speed. He met the jump perfectly, snapping up his knees and rounding his back as he flew over it. I loved jumping him. It was like flying.

I took him over the fence twice more, and then Mom told me to let him have a rest.

"He's looking really good," Soraya said, as I rode out of the ring and halted.

She and Mom started to bustle around, giving his coat a final brush and my boots a final polish. As Mom cleaned his bit with a cloth, I saw Ashley Grant heading over to the ring. A woman with blonde hair was walking beside her. Even from a distance I could hear her giving Ashley instructions.

"I *know* what to do, Mom!" Ashley said sounding irritated.

Soraya noticed them too. "Ashley's in just after you," she said. "I checked on the jumping order."

Mom looked up curiously. "Who are you talking about?"

"Ashley Grant," I said nodding in Ashley's direction. "She's a girl from school."

Mom frowned. "Isn't she from Green Briar?"

I nodded.

"I've heard about that place," Mom said her eyes following Ashley. "I don't like the sound of their methods, though they do get results."

"Well, I'm going to beat her," I said.

"Amy," Mom said, her blue eyes frowning slightly. "That's not the attitude. You should just be thinking about Sundance. As long as you jump a round you're pleased with then you should be happy."

I nodded but exchanged a secret look with Soraya. WE knew differently, of course.

49

I was waiting by the in-gate and watching the competitor before me when I felt a pony walk up beside me. I looked round and saw Ashley.

"Think you're going to get round?" she asked mockingly. "Mules aren't usually known for their jumping ability."

"Sundance is not a mule!" I snapped. Unfortunately, at that moment Sundance decided to do a very accurate mule impression, pinning his ears back and swinging his head up as he objected to Ashley's pony being so close.

"Could have fooled me!" Ashley retorted.

"Number 75 please," the steward by the in-gate called, as the rider in the ring finished the course with one bar down.

"That's me," I said quickly to him.

"See you soon," Ashley drawled. "Probably very soon. I doubt you'll even get over the first jump with that horse!"

The last thing I heard as I trotted through the in-gate was her scornful laugh. "Come on, Sundance," I said, shortening my reins. "We'll show her!"

Sundance moved smoothly forward into a canter and, seeing the jumps, his ears pricked. Energy seemed to be surging through him. I heard the starting buzzer go.

Control, control, I thought, steadying him. Sitting down deep in the saddle I collected him and turned him to the first fence. Suddenly I forgot all about Ashley. Nothing mattered but me and Sundance and the fences in the ring. We reached the first jump. As always, he jumped big but athletically. His knees folded up tight against his body and his back arched. We were safely over it and on to the next. Fence after fence flew by. He met them all on exactly the right stride, changing leads wherever he needed to. I felt like I could go on jumping for ever.

As we soared cleanly over the last, a wave of elation swept through me. Whatever happened, whatever mark we got, I didn't care. Sundance had just jumped the most wonderful round and I was never going to forget it. Patting him hard, I rode towards the in-gate to the sound of applause and then I saw Ashley. There was a look of shocked surprise on her face.

"Great round," the steward at the gate said as he let me out. "Your pony sure can jump."

"He's the best," I said in delight. I met Ashley's eyes. "Give me a mule any day," I said, and ignoring the steward's puzzled expression, I rode away, a grin almost splitting my face in two.

"That was brilliant!" Soraya cried, hurrying up to me and patting Sundance.

"Well done, honey," Mom said, hugging me as I dismounted. "That's the best I've ever seen you and Sundance go."

"He was just perfect," I said, kissing him.

"Your friend's in the ring now," Mom said.

I turned to the ring. Ashley was just jumping the first jump. Her pony, Otto, cleared the fence in a very flashy manner.

"They're good," Soraya said, sounding almost disappointed.

I nodded. Otto was approaching the second jump. When he was a few strides away he seemed to catch sight of a pot of flowers at the side of the jump. He shied abruptly and Ashley lost a stirrup. Otto swung round away from the jump. Within a few paces Ashley had stopped him and turned him back on-course. He jumped the fence.

"Does it matter that he stopped like that?" Soraya asked Mom.

"The judge will certainly penalize it," Mom said, "but how harshly will probably depend on how he jumps the rest of the course. If it's just a one-off then. . ."

Before she could finish her sentence, Otto shied again at the next jump. Mom shook her head. "That's his chance of a ribbon gone. There's no way a judge will place a pony that's shied twice for no real good reason. It shows a nervous, dishonest attitude — not what you want in a hunter pony."

Ashley finally rode out of the ring after Otto had shied four times. Her cheeks were red.

Soraya looked at me quizzically. "Are you going to say anything to her?"

I smiled as I shook my head. I had proved my point in the show ring.

The speakers round the ring crackled. "And the winner of Class 36, Large Pony Hunter, is Amy Fleming riding Sundance!" the announcer said.

The crowd started to clap and I rode Sundance into the ring. Mom and Soraya were standing by the in-gate, clapping and cheering. I couldn't stop smiling. Sundance seemed to know the applause was for him. Arching his neck, he stepped out proudly, his ears pricked.

"You have a lovely pony," the judge said, presenting me with a double-tiered blue ribbon. "Well done!"

"Thank you very much," I said in delight.

As the judge walked down the line of winners handing out the ribbons, I patted Sundance's neck and looked around. As I looked at everyone clapping I could hardly believe that it was only five months since Mom had bought Sundance at the sale.

"I like your pony," the girl in second place said to me.

I smiled at her. "Thanks."

"He's not for sale, is he?" she asked. "My dad's looking for another hunter pony for me."

For sale? "No, no, he's not," I said quickly. As the words left my mouth I felt a shiver run down my spine. Of course! How could I not have thought about it before? Mom rehomed all the horses who came to Heartland once they were cured. Maybe now Sundance had won a blue ribbon and proved he was better, Mom would find a new home for him too. *No*, I thought quickly. *She can't.*

"Are you OK?" the girl next to me said.

I realized that I must be staring at her in horror. "Yeah, yeah, I'm fine," I said quickly.

To my relief, just then the ringmaster asked us to do a lap of honour. Leading the other ribbon winners around the ring at a canter, I forced a smile on my face, but inside I was feeling sick. What would I do if Sundance left Heartland? I didn't think I could bear it.

As I rode out of the ring, I thought to myself that I had to talk to Mom. I had to persuade her to let me keep Sundance. As I rode over I saw that she was talking to a man. Soraya was standing beside them.

"So your daughter wants a pony?" Mom was saying to the man.

"No!" the words burst out of me.

They all looked round.

"Mom, please!" I begged, jumping off Sundance. "Please don't rehome Sundance."

Mom looked at the man. "Would you excuse me a moment, please?"

He nodded, and she came over to me.

"Amy. . ." she began gently.

"Please, Mom," I broke in. "I know we rehome horses when they get better but not Sundance. I love him so much."

Sundance nuzzled my arm, his lips reaching for the ribbon I was still holding in my hand.

"And he loves you." Mom smiled. "Amy, I wasn't planning on rehoming him. The man I'm talking to has got a young daughter who's heard of Heartland. He wanted to see if we had any small ponies who need new homes."

"Oh," I said feeling the breath rush out of me in relief.

Mom shook her head. "I wouldn't take Sundance away from you, honey. You've worked so hard with him. You deserve to keep him." She squeezed my hand. "Sundance is your pony now."

"Oh, Mom! Thank you!" I cried, hugging her.

She turned away from me to go back to the man. Soraya hurried over. "So you're allowed to keep him?" she said eagerly.

"For ever!" I said in delight. "Did you hear that, Sundance?" I said turning to the little pony beside me. "You're mine – all mine." I kissed him on the nose.

Sundance snorted happily in reply.

Chapter Six

How I Discovered T-Touch

The summer I was thirteen, we began to use T-Touch therapy at Heartland. Mom had been on a week-long course run by Linda Tellington-Jones, a renowned horse expert who had first developed T-Touch. When Mom got back from the course she taught me and Ty how to do it.

"Stand like this," Mom told us. "Get really close in to Pegasus's side."

Ty pushed back his untidy dark hair and moved forward until he was standing close to Pegasus's dappled hindquarters. I stood beside him.

"Now put your right hands against his body," Mom instructed. "Cup your fingers slightly so that your palms just skim his hair."

"What do we do with our left hand?" I asked.

"Just rest it against his side," Mom said. "It's your right hand that matters. Now, it's very important that you are relaxed when you do T-Touch, so first of all, I want you both to just breathe for a few moments and focus on Pegasus. Breathe in for a count of five seconds, then breathe out for a count of five. Come on, breathe in. . ."

Ty and I both breathed in but just as I'd reached the count of five, I caught his eye. He was frowning hard in concentration. He looked so funny that I couldn't stop myself. I snorted with laughter.

"Amy, come on," Mom said. "You can't do T-Touch unless you're relaxed. Now focus on Pegasus and breathe."

Avoiding Ty's eyes in case I cracked up again, I breathed in and out as she instructed. Gradually the giggly feeling left me and I started to feel calm and relaxed.

"Now, I want you to move your right hand in a circle," Mom told us. "Push the skin under your fingers in a clockwise direction – don't dig your fingers into his muscles, the idea is to ease the skin over the muscles. Go round for a circle and a quarter, then lift your fingers and do another circle in another spot. It's really

56

important that you don't keep doing the circles in the same spot.'"

We did as she said.

"Good," Mom said approvingly. "Keep your fingers soft, and breathe into the circles as you make them. Try again, and this time really try and feel what his skin is telling you. Let your instincts guide your hands to wherever the circles are needed. It's like listening with your fingers."

I concentrated hard. Shutting my eyes, I tried to do what Mom had said. As I focused on the circles, I felt my hands naturally move to new places on Pegasus's side. I did a circle, then let my fingers move again.

"That's great!" Mom said after a few more minutes.

I opened my eyes. "What do these circles do? I asked.

"They can be used for all sorts of things," Mom replied. "They help relax a horse, they can relieve stress and tension, speed up the healing process and most importantly of all they help you develop a closer relationship with the horse. They really work. I saw it happen so often when I was on the course – horses who were stressed and tense started to relax, and horses who were timid started to bond with their riders. It seems to help so many problems, and it's so easy!'"

"But it's not massage," Ty said.

"No," Mom answered. "If you were massaging you'd be pushing much harder. You can do firmer T-Touch circles if you are working with a laid-back horse or a lazy horse, but generally you should try to keep the touch fairly light."

I tried a few more circles. "Does it matter how fast you go?"

Mom nodded. "If you've got a very tense horse then you'd use quick, light circles until he starts to calm down. To help heal and really relax a horse you slow the circles right down so that each one takes about three seconds to complete."

"And what about where you do them?" Ty asked. "Can you do them anywhere on the horse?"

"The face is the most sensitive area," Mom said. "So that's always a good starting point. You can do the forehead, the ears, the muzzle, even the gums, and then work down over the body. Working on the tail is also particularly good because it helps free tension and rebalance the horse mentally and physically. From now on when you groom a horse I'd like you both to try and find time to do a little bit of T-Touch with it. Is that OK?"

"Sure," Ty said. "If it helps develop a good relationship with a horse then I'll definitely do it."

"Me too," I agreed.

"Excellent," Mom smiled. "Now, why don't you go and bring Sundance and Jasmine in from the field and have a go with them before you ride them? I'll be around if you've got any questions."

Ty and I walked up to the paddock together.

"So what do you think about this T-Touch stuff?" Ty asked curiously.

"It's great," I said, wondering what Sundance would think when I tried it out on him. "And if makes a difference like Mom says, then I'll do it."

Ty nodded. "You know that's what I like best about working here. Your mom is always so open to new ideas. We're always learning new things."

58

"Well, you know what she says," I told him. "A good horseman. . ."

"Never stops learning," Ty completed the sentence and we grinned at each other. Ty had been working at Heartland at the weekends and in the vacations for eighteen months now, and I really liked having him around. He was as into horses as I was and it was fun having him to talk to and ride with.

We reached the gate and called the ponies. They trotted over to us and we buckled up their halters.

"Come on then, you two," Ty said. "Let's go and see what you make of T-Touch."

Sundance and Jasmine seemed to really like the T-Touch circles. I started off working on Sundance's forehead and moved on to his ears and then his muzzle. His head dropped lower and his eyes started to close.

"Look," I said to Ty. "He loves it."

"Jasmine too," Ty said, nodding towards Jasmine who was standing just like Sundance. "I'm going to do her tail now."

Mom came over and showed us some other things to do with their tails as well as making the circles. "Hold the tail out and put your hand underneath it near the top. And now push upwards so that you're pushing the bone into an arc, then circle the tail in different directions," she said, demonstrating with Jasmine. "It will help to make the horse more aware of his hindquarters, and if you do this –" she gently slid her hands down Jasmine's tail, pulling back as she did so "– it helps release tension in his back and opens up the spine." As I moved to take hold of Sundance's tail, Mom caught me by the shoulders and moved me to one side of him. "Even when you're doing this, remember never to stand directly behind the horse, Amy. Always stand slightly to one side in case he kicks out," she reminded me.

I nodded.

"And watch out for them sighing or taking a breath," Mom said. "That's a sign that what you're doing is working."

She left us again. After we had worked their tails, we gave them a quick brush over and then tacked up and rode out on the trail that led up Teak's Hill.

"You know," Ty said thoughtfully, after we had been riding five minutes. "Jasmine feels more relaxed."

"I was just thinking the same thing about Sundance," I said. "His back seems to be swinging more – it feels freer."

"Jasmine's too," Ty said. He patted her black neck. "All those circles and tail-pulling must have worked."

"I wonder what else T-Touch can do," I said.

When we got back to Heartland, Mom was standing on the yard with her car keys in her hand. "I've just had a call from Dianne Owen," she told us.

Dianne ran a small horse-breeding farm on Wilson's Peak.

"She's having a problem with one of her foals," Mom continued "An eight-month-old filly who wants her own way all the time. I thought I might go up there and take a look. Do you two want to come?"

"Sure!" I said, jumping off Sundance. I loved visiting Dianne's well-kept yard and seeing all her wonderful mares and foals.

60

"Me too," Ty said quickly. "I'll just get Jasmine untacked."

As soon as Sundance and Jasmine had been untacked and brushed, we drove over. It was only twenty minutes away and as we pulled up in front of the house, Dianne, a small cheerful woman in her fifties, came out to meet us.

"Hi, guys," she said to me and Ty, then she smiled at Mom. "Thanks for coming over so soon, Marion."

"No problem," Mom replied. "Where's this foal then?"

"This way." Dianne led us up the yard to a large field. "That's Ruby," she said, pointing to a chestnut foal that was standing on her own.

As we watched, the foal's dark eyes flickered across the paddock to where three other youngsters were grazing. With no warning, she suddenly pinned her ears back, and charged. The other foals skittered away, kicking their heels in protest. Looking smug, the filly lowered her head to tear at the patch of grass they had been eating.

"There she goes," Dianne said, a sigh in her voice. "Getting what she wants as usual." She looked at Mom. "She doesn't seem to respect anyone or anything. It takes me for ever to catch her, she barges when I lead her, she kicks out when she's eating or if I try and groom her." She shook her head. "You know my beliefs, Marion. I like to think that if you handle horses with respect they'll respond accordingly. But not Ruby. She just seems determined to do what she wants."

Mom looked at the chestnut foal. "Let's get her in and I'll see what she's like."

"If she'll be caught," Dianne said. She picked a halter from a hook by the gate and went into the field. "Ruby!" The foal looked up but didn't move. Dianne walked towards her. "Here, baby."

Ruby cantered away.

Dianne rummaged in her pocket and pulled out some mints. "Here, girl."

Ruby stopped and looked at her. Her ears pricked but as soon as Dianne came close, she tossed her head and trotted away.

Dianne turned back to the gate. "This is what she always does. I end up following her round for ages."

"Here, I'll try," Mom said. "Amy, have you got any horse cookies with you?"

I nodded and rummaging in my pockets, dug out a few pieces. "What are you going to do, Mom? Join-up with her?"

Mom usually did this when a horse was being difficult to catch – chasing it away until it asked to be allowed to come close.

"Isn't this field too big for join-up?" Ty asked.

Mom nodded. "Yes it is, Ty. I'd end up walking round the field after her all afternoon. No I'll have to try something else." Mom looked at Dianne. "Can we take the other foals in? Most youngsters hate being on their own. If the others are in the barn, then maybe Ruby will stop thinking it's quite so much fun out here."

Dianne nodded. "Sure."

We caught and haltered the other foals. After they had been safely put into their barn, Mom walked back to the paddock. Ruby was trotting up and down by the gate whinnying. But as soon as Mom walked towards her, she wheeled away.

"OK, girl," Mom said with a shrug. "If that's the way you want to play it."

She turned round and came back to us. She'd barely got five paces down the yard when Ruby trotted to the gate and whinnied. Mom ignored her. "I'm just going to leave her for ten minutes," she said to us.

Dianne looked confused. "But she's by the gate. I'm sure we could trap her between us."

"But that's not the point. I want her to come in willingly," Mom replied. "I'm going to give her the choice. She can choose to be caught and get what she wants – which is to join the other foals in the barn – or she can choose to run away, in which case she'll stay out here on her own. It's much better if you can get a horse to cooperate willingly with you rather than forcing it to do what you want – it makes your relationship with it much stronger in the end."

We sat down on a grassy bank and waited. Every so often, Mom would go up to the field. If Ruby trotted away Mom would just shrug and turn round and come back to us, leaving Ruby looking indignantly after her.

At long last, Ruby finally seemed to figure out what was going on. When Mom opened the gate for about the tenth time, the foal stood still and looked at her mutinously. "Hey there, Ruby," Mom murmured.

Ruby hesitated and then suddenly she gave in and walked over. Mom fed her a horse cookie and slipped on the halter.

As she led the filly through the gate, Ruby set her shoulder and began to barge down the yard.

Mom quickly stopped her. "You don't get to go to the barn if you act like that," she said. And quietly but firmly she led Ruby back to the gate and started again. Every time Ruby tried to barge, Mom simply turned her round and made her go back to the gate. After ten minutes of being turned around and led back to the gate, the little foal suddenly seemed to realize that pulling wasn't going to get her where she wanted to go. With a sigh, she gave in and walked calmly all the way down to the barn.

As Mom set Ruby free with the other foals, Dianne joined her. "What do I do with her?" she said despairingly. "She's a nightmare, isn't she?"

Mom looked at the little filly. "Well, she's not easy, that's for sure. The trouble is that although most horses want to be told what to do and to have a leader to follow, Ruby doesn't. She's the sort of horse who would be a lead mare in a herd — she's very dominant and very stubborn. There's no point in trying to use force with a horse like Ruby, she'll only fight you. What you need to do is give her choices like I just did. Show her that if she cooperates with you then her life will be much easier and more pleasant."

Dianne nodded. "I like the idea. Though I guess it takes patience."

"Plenty of it," Mom smiled. She looked at Ruby. "You could also try working her with T-Touch. Have you heard of it?"

Dianne shook her head.

"Let's give Ruby ten minutes with the other foals, then I'll show you what I mean," Mom told her. She smiled at me and Ty. "Looks like you're going to get to see how T-Touch can be used to help a difficult horse," she said.

Ten minutes later, Mom had tied Ruby up to a hitching rail and was demonstrating T-Touch circles. Ruby looked uncertain, her head was high and her muscles tense.

"With Ruby, the first thing you need to do is to get her to relax and accept your touch," Mom told us. "So you need to use quick light anti-clockwise circles on her shoulder and hindquarters."

Mom demonstrated what she meant. As her fingers moved lightly and confidently over the filly's neck and shoulder, the wariness gradually started to leave Ruby's eyes.

"Now she's looking a little less tense I'm going to slow the circles down and, working clockwise, try and get her to relax even more," Mom explained after ten minutes.

She began to move her fingers more slowly. Working her way up Ruby's neck, she took hold of the halter. "Doing circles between the eyes and up to the ears is great for horses who are tense," she said. As her hands worked on Ruby's forehead. Ruby sighed and lowered her head. Mom moved down to work around her mouth, making tiny circles on Ruby's lips and gums. "Horses who are resistant and stubborn often hold a lot of tension around their mouths," she said. "If you work the tension away then you should find them becoming more manageable. Though obviously you can't do this with a horse who might bite."

Within fifteen minutes, Ruby's eyes were starting to shut. "I've never seen her so relaxed!" Dianne said in astonishment. "It's amazing!"

"Here, you have a try," Mom said to her.

They swapped places. Ruby's eyes flickered open at the change of handler but within a few minutes of Dianne's fingers starting to work in T-Touch circles, the tension left the filly and she started to relax again.

"Her eyes look really soft," Ty said.

I nodded. When we'd first seen Ruby in the field, I'd noticed that her expression was hard and proud, but now her eyes were like soft dark pools and her ears were hanging loosely.

"Why don't you have a try at leading her back to the barn?" Mom said to Dianne. "If she barges, stop her, bring her back, work on her with T-Touch until she's relaxed, and then try again."

Dianne untied Ruby. The foal walked quietly for a few paces, but then she saw where she was heading and she began to pull.

"Stop her now!" Mom called quickly.

Dianne brought Ruby back to the hitching post, tied her up again and then, just as Mom had suggested, worked her with T-Touch circles until her head had lowered again. This time, when Ruby was untied, she sighed and then walked quietly all the way to the barn.

"That's incredible!" Dianne exclaimed as she shut the gate after her. "I've never got her to walk as quietly as that before! You're a miracle-worker, Marion."

Mom smiled. "There are no miracles in horse training. You just need plenty of time, patience and a willingness to take a look at things from the horse's point of view. The important thing is not to fight with Ruby, because if you do she'll only fight back. Let her feel that she's choosing to do what you want rather than being forced to do it. That way you'll develop a relationship with her based on mutual trust and respect — and that's the best kind of relationship of all." She turned to me and Ty. "Well, come on you two. There are horses at home who will be wanting their supper."

We said goodbye to Dianne and started walking towards the car. Suddenly I heard a shrill whinny. Ruby had come to the barn gate and was staring after Mom. Her nostrils were flared, her eyes were wide.

Ty smiled at Mom. "I bet if she could talk, she'd be saying *you understand me, I want to be your friend*," he said to Mom.

Mom smiled back. "I hope you're right. I like to feel that I can show horses that there are humans who will listen and respect them, who can be friends as well as leaders. In the end, all that most horses want is someone to depend on and trust."

I tucked my arm through hers. "Someone like you."

"Not just me," Mom said seriously. "There are only so many horses I can help myself, and that's why I need to teach other people what I know. By showing other people how to develop a true, rewarding partnership with a horse, based on trust and respect, then I can help far more horses than just the ones who come to Heartland. If I tell people what I know, then hopefully they will use that knowledge and pass it on." She looked at Ty and me. "If everyone who cares about horses work together, then maybe we'll eventually make the world a better place for all horses."

"I'd like that," Ty said.

I smiled at him and Mom. "Me too," I said.

Chapter Seven

Newspaper Cuttings

Hitting the Big Time

Many teenagers who own a horse and ride in local shows dream of one day hitting the big time. For one lucky eighteen year-old at Marriott Park, Virginia, that dream finally came true.

"I'm just amazed," Marion Bartlett told us as she patted her bay thoroughbred mare, Delilah, after collecting the blue ribbon in the $10, 000 High Junior/Amateur-Open Jumper Classic. "I can't believe we did it!"

Bartlett lives on her parents' farm just fifteen miles away in North Virginia. Having been a self-professed "pony-mad" kid, she bought an unbroken four-year-old for 250 dollars at the age of fourteen, with money earned from washing cars and babysitting. In making that purchase, she took the first step towards her dream.

"No one wanted Delilah," Bartlett said. "She was half-wild and known to buck, so the owner sold her cheaply. I spent ages with her until she had quietened down enough for me to get on. She was the best purchase I ever made."

Bartlett credits her success to her parents, who have instilled in her the value of hard work and persistence. "Dad's always told me that if you want something then you have to work for it – and that's what I've done with Delilah. In the early days she had me on the floor almost every time I rode her and she used to jump out of her field at least once a week, but I kept trying with her and last year, when she hit seven, she just seemed to turn good."

Delilah certainly did. Out of the last ten classes they have entered, Bartlett and Delilah have been placed in every one.

Bartlett has her feet firmly on the ground though. "It's a humbling sport," she said. "You can have a great round one day and knock all the bars flying the next. I'm not going to get too excited. I'm just going to take one show at a time."

When asked about her future dreams, a smile lights up Bartlett's blue eyes. "To compete for the US, of course," she says. And travel? "Yes, I'd love to see Europe and maybe jump over there," Bartlett replies. "So long as I'm riding horses I don't care what I do." She gives a little shrug. "I'll just have to see what the future holds."

If Bartlett's performance at Meadowville is anything to go by it looks as though her future's going to be very bright indeed.

Wedded Bliss

On 2nd July, Virginian-born, Marion Bartlett, 21, married British showjumper, Tim Fleming, 23, at St Mary's Church, Meadowville, Virginia. A veteran of the international showjumping circuit since his junior days, Gloucestershire-based Fleming met Bartlett when she spent last summer in Europe competing on her bay mare, Delilah. The couple were engaged at Christmas.

The small church service was attended by family and friends. The bride wore a simple sleeveless white dress with a full skirt and was given away by her father, Jack. The reception was held at the bride's parents' house.

After a honeymoon in Argentina, the happy couple will be returning to their showjumping yard in Gloucestershire, England. They both plan to continue competing.

Clean Sweep for Fleming

Tim Fleming and Pegasus achieved a clean sweep at the Horse of the Year show in London, England, winning the Grand Prix on the final day of this competition to add to his impressive wins in the International Jumping Stakes and the Six-Bar earlier in the week.

There were 35 starters in the Grand Prix but Toby Anderson's course proved challenging with many horses taking exception to the final element of the triple combination, a high vertical. Out of the 35 starters only five horses went clear. Pegasus, an eleven-year-old English Thoroughbred, made it look easy.

Fleming bought the versatile dapple-grey gelding as a four-year-old from a hunting stable. "There was just something about him," Fleming said, "a look in his eyes that I liked. We seemed to click from day one. He's strong to ride but as brave as they come." Seven years later, Fleming and Pegasus are a perfect study in the benefits of a long-term partnership.

Fleming went first in the jump-off and turning in tightly before the double and pushing for just five strides between fences five and six, clocked a time of 35.6 seconds. It was to prove unbeatable. Jan Taylor came closest with a lovely round of 39.3 which put her and her bay stallion, Albatross, into second place.

Married to USA rider, Marion Fleming, née Bartlett, Fleming has his sights firmly set on the World Championships in August next year. "The World Championships are definitely my goal at the moment," he explained. "Pegasus is a fairly young horse for such a challenge but he always rises to the big occasions. We've been in several Nations' Cup teams now and Pegasus has always done what's needed. He's truly a show horse and if I have my way, we'll be there."

If Tim Fleming's performance this week is anything to go by then there are few who'll bet against him achieving his goal.

Team Fleming

Tim and Marion Fleming are best known as showjumping's golden couple, and now their talent seems to be shining through to the next generation. Last month, *Horse Life*'s Sarah Johns, caught up with the family at their yard in Gloucestershire. . .

Since first competing as a junior for Britain in the European Championships, Tim Fleming, 35, has rarely been out of showjumping spotlight. Partnerships with horses such as Mesmerize, Tennison and now his popular dapple-grey, Pegasus, have kept him at the forefront of the sport. His list of triumphs is formidable – winner of the individual silver in the last European championships, winner of the Hickstead Derby, the King George V Cup, the Oslo Grand Prix, the Puissance at Olympia, to name but a few, as well as being a crucial member of Britain's last two successful Nation's Cup Teams.

Tim's Virginian-born wife, Marion, 33, is also well known for her showjumping ability. She shot on to the international scene when she was just twenty, by winning the prestigious Queen Elizabeth II cup at the Royal International Horse Show, Hickstead, England on her bay mare, Delilah. She now likes to concentrate on bringing on the young horses at the couple's showjumping yard, teaching students and looking after the couple's two daughters, eleven-year-old Lou and two-year-old Amy.

Visiting the family on their yard deep in the heart of the Gloucestershire countryside, it is clear that they share a great sense of camaraderie. All the family members help out with the horses. When I arrive, even Amy, at just two years old, is out on the yard busy trying to brush Pegasus' tail. The powerful grey gelding, known for his boldness and athletic strength in the ring, stands as quietly as a thirty-year-old pony as Amy, a skinny, dark-blonde toddler dressed in pink dungarees moves fearlessly around his great hooves while Marion keeps a careful eye on proceedings.

"Amy's first word was horse," she smiles when I comment on Amy's confidence. "When she was a baby I used to carry her round in a sling with me as I oversaw the yard and taught lessons. She's been riding since she was twelve months old. One day just after her first birthday, she saw her dad and sister going out for a ride and just started pointing and saying, 'horse, horse'. We had a special saddle from when Lou learned to ride. We put Amy in that on Lou's old pony, Minnie and that was it. She's been riding ever since."

Just then, Tim and Lou come down the yard to say hello. They make a contrasting pair. Lou, small and slim, has Marion's corn-coloured hair and blue eyes while Tim is tall and dark. But the love between them is obvious. As they walk down the yard, they are laughing together about a jumping lesson Tim has just been giving Lou.

"Dad had me jumping without stirrups and I fell off twice!" Lou tells me with a giggle. Although her cream jodhpurs bear the marks of her fall, she appears unfazed. "At least it's one less time than yesterday," she says with a grin.

Lou is clearly a chip off the old block. After competing in pony club events when she was younger, she started in affiliated competitions a year ago. Since then she has been winning regularly on her lively chestnut pony, Nugget. "I can't stop him at all," she tells me. "He's like a tank. I just point him at the fences and let him go." I glance at Tim and see that he is smiling proudly.

With twenty-five horses in work and another five home-bred youngsters to be looked after each day, the Fleming family's daily routine is hectic to say the least. They have three grooms who are all treated as part of the family. Head groom, Sally Henson, has been with the family for seven years now and is in charge of organizing the yard's busy show schedule. "We couldn't manage without Sally," Marion says. "I'm useless at paperwork."

"We'd end up at all the wrong shows if it was left to Mum!" Lou grins.

Tim kisses his wife's head. "You're wonderful at other things."

Amy throws her arms around Marion's knees.

Marion smiles. "OK, now I feel loved," she laughs.

It is clear that one of the family's secrets of success is their support of each other. When I ask Tim about his ambitions for the future, he tells me that the World Championships in August is his next goal, followed by the Olympics. And will he be going for gold? "What else?" he says, his grey eyes narrowing slightly and for the first time I see a glimpse of the gritty determination that has led to him heading the line-ups in so many major classes. Tim Fleming may be a devoted father and husband, but make no mistake, underneath his calm, easy-going exterior there is a steely will to win. The other competitors in the World Championships in Stockholm better watch out. Team Fleming are on their way.

Tragic Accident at World Championships

Showjumping honours at the World Championships in Stockholm, Sweden, belonged to Germany, who took the team championship from the French with the USA in bronze-medal position. However, the results of the championship sank into insignificance after a dreadful fall in the final round of yesterday's individual competition left British rider, Tim Fleming, in hospital in a critical condition.

On target for a double clear, Fleming turned sharply into the final fence – a wide oxer. His horse, the well-known grey, Pegasus, attempted to take off but he was too close to the fence to clear it properly and he caught the top bar between his front legs. Somersaulting over, Pegasus landed on Fleming.

Fleming, 36, was rushed to a local hospital and was later transferred to a specialist spinal injuries unit. His wife, showjumper, Marion, and his twelve-year-old daughter, Louise, are at his bedside. Youngest daughter, Amy, aged three, is at home in England. Fleming's condition is not thought to be life-threatening. However, at the moment, doctors are unable to say whether he will ever ride again.

The atmosphere at the show is one of shock. A very popular rider, Tim has been competing internationally for twenty years, first as a junior and then as an adult. "It just puts everything into perspective," Mark Crooks, one of the American team, said. "It happened so quickly. I was talking to Tim just before he went in and now he's in hospital. It makes you realize how fragile everything is. I just hope Tim's going to be OK." His sentiment was echoed by all.

Horse Whisperer?

If there's one thing that Marion Fleming's learned in the four years since she founded Heartland, an equine sanctuary set deep in the heart of North Virginia, it's that there's far more to working with troubled horses than simply whispering to horses. "Working with horses who are traumatized and have suffered abuse, you need endless patience, persistence, respect and, most of all, a willingness to listen to the horse," she says. These are qualities that Fleming has in abundance. A former top showjumper, she returned to her childhood home in Virginia five years ago after her marriage broke up, and a year later, she started Heartland on her father's land. "I find it a real challenge working with traumatized horses," she says. "And if I can help those horses who everyone else has given up on, then so much the better."

Marion is no stranger to trauma in her own life. When she was just 21, her mother, Alice, died of cancer, only six months after Marion had married. "I was pregnant at the time," Marion recalls quietly. "It's always been one of my greatest regrets that my mom never knew her granddaughters." Five years ago, Marion's then-husband, British showjumper, Tim Fleming, was involved in a dreadful accident at the Showjumping World Championships in Stockholm. The accident left him temporarily paralysed and unable to compete again. The Flemings' marriage broke up under the strain and, seven months later, Marion returned to Virginia. She now lives with her father, Jack Bartlett, a retired dairy farmer, and Amy, her eight-year-old daughter. Marion and Tim's oldest daughter, Lou, aged sixteen, has chosen to stay on at her English boarding school and splits her time between England and Virginia. "It's hard having Lou living away from home," Marion says, "but it was what she wanted and I respected her decision."

Using natural remedies to complement conventional veterinary medicine, Marion heals horses who have no other place to go and then finds them new, loving homes. "I learnt about alternative therapies by looking after Pegasus after the accident. He had a chip in his front knee and he was traumatized mentally. Conventional medicine only helped a certain amount and so I started looking for other ways to heal him. Using herbs, aromatherapy and Bach Flower Remedies really seemed to make a difference to his condition and the more I learned, the more interested I became. A year after I moved back home I decided to use my new knowledge to start helping other horses as well and so Heartland began."

In the last four years, Heartland has become increasingly well-known and Marion has just had a new twelve-stall barn built. "People have started to hear about my work and ask me to help them with their horses," she explains. "I hope to do that by having more space to take in boarders who have behavioural problems. The fees their owners will pay will help to finance the rescue side of my work."

Looking around the peaceful yard, it is a sobering thought that many of Heartland's equine inhabitants would no longer be alive if it hadn't been for Marion and her undoubted skills. Once branded as rogue or dangerous, these horses now graze peacefully in the green fields and wait to be rehomed with loving owners, all carefully vetted by Marion herself. Marion has worked miracles with these horses and anyone who cares abut equine welfare can only hope that a place like Heartland will continue to go from strength to strength.

Winning Streak

Local rider, Amy Fleming, 13, was on a winning streak when she carried off the large pony championship at Meadowville, Virginia, on her buckskin pony, Sundance.

Fleming won both over-fences classes on the first day although Ashley Grant's Watch Me gave Fleming and Sundance a run for their money. The chestnut and Grant were the first to tackle the course and they did so in style. Their scores held throughout the whole large pony division until Fleming entered the ring. Spectators could see Fleming talking to the ten-year-old Sundance as they cantered a circle before the first jump.

"I was bribing him with promises of horse cookies as we went in," Fleming grins when questioned. Whatever she was saying certainly seemed to work. Sundance jumped a near flawless round in both classes.

"He was incredible!" Fleming enthused afterwards. "I just let him do his own thing and he flew round." Fleming is trained at her home, Heartland, by her mom, ex-showjumper Marion Fleming. For both of them, Sundance's victory was especially sweet. Only eighteen months ago, the buckskin had been headed for a slaughter sale, but then the Flemings bought him at auction and turned him into a show pony.

"He's not the easiest of ponies," Amy admitted. "But he's an incredible jumper. He jumps high and wide and can make a jump look great from any distance." She smiles. "I wouldn't swap him for the world."

Chapter Eight

Alternative Remedies

We use loads of herbs at Heartland. Here are my five favourites:

Comfrey

Comfrey is a large-leafed green plant that grows in hedgerows, woodlands and meadows. It is also called "Knitbone" and is excellent for treating tendon strains and bone-damage, for example, splints, arthritis and fractures. Ty and I used it to help Jigsaw, an ex-riding school pony who had a stress fracture in one front leg. She healed really well. I also gave it to Sundance when he strained his tendon. Horses usually love to eat comfrey. The purple and pink-flowered types are generally the best because they won't excite the horse. You can feed both the leaves and the root (though you have to clean the root first and you mustn't feed a horse the root for too long). The amount you feed depends on the size of your horse and what is wrong with it – you need to check this out in a herbal book like *A Modern Horse Herbal* by Hilary Page Self. When Sundance strained his tendon, I fed him six medium-sized leaves for ten days. You can also buy comfrey ointment, which is great for speeding up the healing process of small wounds.

Fenugreek Seeds

Fenugreek seeds contain lots of vitamins and are rich in calcium. They help improve your horse's general condition and will increase his appetite. I used them to tempt Sugarfoot, the Shetland, to eat when he was pining for his old owner. You need to feed about 20–30 grams of the seed a day. It goes very well with garlic; the two herbs seem to bring out the best in each other.

Garlic

Garlic will make your horse's breath smell but it's awesome stuff! It protects horses from infection, is good for the heart and blood and respiratory system. It acts as a fly repellent, and relieves Sweet Itch. For a horse of about 15 hands, add two crushed cloves of fresh garlic to their feed per day, or buy dried garlic as a feed supplement and give the amount it says on the tub. It's not so good for young foals because it can upset their digestion – that's why I didn't give it to Daybreak, Melody's foal, when she had a respiratory virus. But it's great for most horses. We feed it a lot.

Mint

All the horses love peppermints and most love the taste of fresh mint too! If you've got a horse who is a fussy eater then just add a handful of mint leaves or 15–20 grams of dried mint to their feed each day and watch them start eating!

Valerian

Valerian is great for calming horses down without affecting their performance. It's good for show horses and for horses who are nervous or stressed. You can buy powdered valerian, which you add to the horse's feed. It smells quite strong, so be warned! Sometimes it's good to combine it with Skullcap, which is another herb, which also helps calms horses down without making them sleepy.

Chapter Nine
Aromatherapy and Other Remedies

Aromatherapy works with people and animals. We use it for lots of things at Heartland, for example, to help horses who are sad or traumatized, to calm stressed horses, and to treat physical problems like tendon strains.

It's really important to buy good quality oils and you must make sure you buy essential oils, not just scented oils. Essential oils are very strong and before you can use them on a horse you have to dilute them in a base oil. If you used them full strength they might burn or irritate the horse. We use sweet almond oil as a base oil at Heartland. What we do is put 10 mls of sweet almond oil in a dark bottle and then add up to eight drops of essential oil. You can add up to four types of essential oil to one bottle of sweet almond oil but you mustn't add more than a total of eight drops of essential oils to the 10 mls of base oil unless a properly-qualified aromatherapist tells you otherwise.

There are lots of different oils to choose from. One of the best things about working with essential oils is that the horse helps you decide how to treat it – you just have to listen to what your horse says. To choose which is right for your horse look in an aromatherapy book to find a selection of oils that might be appropriate for your horse's problem, for example if your horse spooks a lot you might want to offer him a choice between jasmine oil, clary sage oil, violet leaf oil, roman camomile oil and vetiver oil, which are all oils that are good for nervousness. Open the bottles and offer the oils to the horse one at a time. Hold on to the bottle tightly so the horse can't grab it, and hold it just beneath his nostrils. If the oil will help the horse the horse will look interested and may even try and reach to take the bottle (be careful he doesn't succeed, and don't let his nose actually touch the bottle in case the oil irritates his skin!). If the oil isn't going to help, then the horse will turn his head away or ignore it. Always work with your horse and listen to him. It's amazing how horses seem to be able to tell which oils will help them.

Once you've chosen the oils you are going to use, you need to dilute them in a base oil and then you can apply them. The best way is to massage them into the horse's muzzle and into the underside of his neck (but don't get the oils near his eyes). If your horse has a tendon strain or muscle aches, then you can massage the oil directly into his sore muscles. We usually apply oils twice a day at Heartland. You should notice an improvement in four or five days. If there is no improvement then try a different oil.

There are a few things to be careful of when using essential oils – don't use aromatherapy with in-foal mares and if it is very sunny, it is best to wait until the evening before applying oils to a horse's muzzle because otherwise the horse's muzzle may get sunburnt. If the symptoms get worse or the horse has an allergic reaction (small lumps appear where you put the oil) then stop applying the oil and consult your vet. Some essential oils have substances in them that are banned when competing under rules and there is a danger that if your horse licks the oils off his coat and is then tested at a competition he might test positive. So if you are competing it is best to stop the use of oils a week before the show, or apply the oils somewhere on the horse where he can't lick them off, e.g. the top of his neck and under his chin.

The oils we use most at Heartland:

Lavender

Lavender has to be my favourite oil. It's very good at soothing nervous or tense horses and for treating horses who are recovering from an illness or a trauma. If you are feeling stressed you can add a few drops of essential lavender oil to a bath, or if you are having problems sleeping put a few drops on a tissue and place it under your pillow. The smell should send you straight off to sleep. I always take some to shows with me. Lavender is also good for helping scars heal. It is a very safe oil and can actually be applied undiluted to the scar.

Tea Tree Oil

Tea tree oil comes from Australia. It kills bacteria and helps cure fungal or viral infections. If you add a few drops to a bucket and use it as a final rinse for your horse it will help soothe any dry skin and keep flies away. Tea tree oil is great for wounds, stings and bites. It helps fight any infection. To use it on open wounds it is best to use it undiluted (like lavender it is a very safe oil) or dilute it in aloe vera gel (adding 10–15 drops of tea tree oil to 50 ml of gel) instead of a base oil, because the base oil might irritate the wound. You can buy ready-made aloe vera and tea tree oil gel. Put some in your first aid kit now!

Pine

For horses who are having a respiratory infection, pine oil is just great. It really helps clear their breathing. For horses who have a cold, we make up a mixture of 2 drops of pine oil, 2 drops of tea tree oil and 2 drops of peppermint oil added to 10 mls of sweet almond oil. We massage this into the horse's outer nostrils and the sides of his face and lower jaw for a week. It really seems to help.

Black Pepper
We use black pepper oil to help treat tendon and muscle injuries and pain. You only need a small amount because it is very strong. I used a mixture of black pepper, lime, eucalyptus and peppermint oils when treating Sundance's strained tendon. A mixture we use a lot at Heartland is: 1 drop of black pepper oil, 1 drop of peppermint and 3 drops of eucalyptus, added to 10 mls of sweet almond oil. Massage your horse's legs quite firmly with this and the stiffness and pain should just melt away.

Neroli
This oil is excellent for grieving, sad or depressed horses. It's particularly good for horses who have lost a companion and I used it on Sugarfoot. If you ever have to deal with a horse who is sad, depressed, unconfident or suffering from loss, massage diluted neroli oil around their nostrils and under their neck and it should help. Neroli oil smells lovely and you can make a rinse for your own hair by adding four drops of it to 500 ml of warm water and then pouring it over your hair on the final rinse after shampooing. Ty loves the smell!

Getting rid of flies:

Feed the horse two crushed cloves of garlic a day and make up this mixture of aromatherapy oils:

    20 drops of lavender oil
    20 drops of tea tree oil
    20 drops of white thyme oil

Shake the oils together in a bottle and add to 200 ml of water in a spray bottle. Shake well and then spray it over your horse. It smells lovely but flies seem to hate it!

To relieve stiff muscles:

This is a great muscle wash. It is good either after exercise or after a long journey:

    20 drops of eucalyptus oil
    20 drops of birch oil
    10 drops of juniper oil
    5 drops of black pepper oil

Add to 750 ml of warm water in a bucket and wash your horse down with it using a sponge. A little shampoo added to the water helps to stop the oils making the coat greasy. It might be an idea to have a trial run at home first to check that your horse is going to look as beautiful as possible in the ring!

Bach Flower Remedies

Bach Flower remedies were developed by Dr Edward Bach in the 1930s. We find them really good for dealing with horses who have emotional problems, such as being scared, tense, depressed or agitated. The remedies come from different plants. They come in little brown bottles and are completely safe and can be used alongside conventional medicine and other alternative remedies. We find they combine particularly well with aromatherapy. The important thing about Bach Flower Remedies is choosing exactly the right remedy for the horse's emotional state. For example, if you've got a fearful horse, then you need to look at the exact nature of the fear and that will help you select the appropriate remedy. So a horse who is showing an extreme state of fear and terror would need Rock Rose, whereas a horse who is generally anxious and nervy would probably be better with Mimulus. A horse who has turned aggressive because of fear might benefit from Cherry Plum and a horse who is scared for another, e.g. a mare scared for her ill foal, would be best with Red Chestnut.

The easiest way to treat a horse with Bach Flower Remedies is to add 10 drops of the chosen remedy into their water bucket, or you can add the drops to a small piece of bread or a chunk of carrot and feed them to the horse directly. You can give up to six different remedies at one time.

Bach Flower Remedies also work really well for people too. If you're nervous before a show or an exam, try taking a few drops of Mimulus each day in the week beforehand (for on-going anxiety about a specific event). If you're the sort of person who panics easily when something goes wrong, you might want to take Elm (for keeping things in perspective) or Gentian (for maintaining confidence) as well. For a person who has had a bad fall and lost their confidence, Rock Rose (for extreme fear) or Larch (for anxiety and lack of confidence) might help.

Rescue Remedy is one of the most useful Bach Flower Remedies. It's brilliant in an emergency. It is made up of five remedies – Rose for panic, Cherry Plum for loss of self-control, Impatiens for tension, Clematis for faintness and Star of Bethlehem for trauma. If a person or horse has had an accident, it is great for helping deal with shock. You should take four drops every twenty minutes for an hour. I always have some in my grooming kit just in case.

My top five folk remedies:
Mom knew lots of strange folk remedies that she picked up on her travels. Here are a few of them:

Cider Vinegar
Cider Vinegar is a very good way of putting a shine on a horse's coat – particularly if you've got a bay, chestnut or black. All you have to do is add 125 ml of cider vinegar in the final bucket of rinsing water that you use when washing your horse. Your horse will really gleam!

Cold Tea
Cold tea is excellent if you've got a horse with sweet itch. Add 500 ml of water to four teabags. Leave for five minutes and remove the

teabags with a spoon. When the tea is cold, apply the tea to the horse's neck, mane and tail. It works brilliantly and stops the horse wanting to scratch!

Cobwebs

This is an old remedy my mom told me about, but I have to say I've never tried it! Apparently people used to use cobwebs to help heal small wounds. You need a clean, newly spun cobweb (not a dusty one) – so get up early and go into the countryside to get one! Place the cobweb over the wound and bandage. Remove the bandage after twenty-four hours. The wound will be healing well, or at least that's what Mom told me. I think it might be best to call the vet instead – at least that way you get to avoid the spiders!

Honey

Honey is great. It seems to calm down excitable horses and re-energize lazy horses. It seems to have a balancing effect, making a difficult horse easier to work with. All you need to do is add a tablespoon of clear honey to your horse's regular feed and wait to see if there's any difference. Ben uses it with Red and it really seems to relax him and keep him calm before a show.

Newspaper

If a horse is cold or suffering from a chill you can warm him up by placing newspaper over his back and hindquarters. Cover with a rug to keep the newspaper in place.

Chapter Ten

Important Stuff

My Mom taught me lots about working with horses. I thought you might like to share some of the things she felt were most important when training a horse.

Listen to the horse.

Most behavioural problems are caused not by the horse being mean-spirited or downright naughty, but because the horse is scared or in pain. If a horse is behaving badly, first have him checked over by a vet to rule out any physical problems such as a sore back, then make sure that his tack fits him well and isn't pinching or rubbing him anywhere, then examine his diet. Are you feeding him a food that will make him hot up (like oats)? If all these causes are ruled out, then start trying to think like your horse, try and find out why he is reacting like he is, what's upsetting him, what he is scared of. If you can find the root of the pain or the fear and take it away, then the horse's behaviour will almost always change for the better.

Training should be based on cooperation not confrontation.

If you try and force a horse to do what you want, you may succeed but you will end up with an unwilling, resentful servant. If you establish a relationship built on mutual trust and respect, then you will have a truly wonderful partnership with your horse that will enrich your life.

A true partnership should be based on mutual respect.

Using kind training techniques does not mean letting your horse do whatever he wants. The important thing is that you can get your horse's respect without resorting to traditional physical domination like smacking and hitting. All you have to do is show your horse he has a choice. He can either choose to do what you want and make his life easy or he can choose to do what he wants and make his life tough. For example, if you've got a horse who barges from the field to the stable like Solitaire, a headstrong foal we had at Heartland, then every time he barges you don't smack him or jerk on the rope, you just stop him, turn him round and take him back to the field gate. You do this as many times as you need until he gets the message that he can either choose to walk quietly to his stall, in which case he will get to the barn like he wants, or he can choose to barge forward in which case he will go back to the field gate. You don't mind which he does (at least that's what you let him think!) – the choice is his. We use this technique all the time at Heartland, often combining it with join-up. For example, if a horse doesn't like having his feet picked up (and we've had him checked out by Scott, our vet, to make sure there's definitely no physical problem), we take him to the circular pen. Then we try and pick his feet up. If he resists then we send him away from us, making him canter round the pen until he offers us a sign that he wants to be friends, then we let him join-up and try lifting his feet up again. If he resists we send him away again. The choice is his. He can either choose to cooperate and have his feet picked up, or he can choose to refuse in which case he's sent off to do some work cantering round the ring. The important thing if you use this technique is that you don't ever get mad, you stay calm and let the horse choose how to behave. You need lots of patience but it's worth it. In the end you will have a true and fulfilling partnership with your horse.

Chapter Eleven
Heartland Recipes

These recipes use American cup measurements – the measurements we use at Heartland. If you don't have a set of measuring cups, don't worry, just use a measuring jug.

1 cup – 250 ml
½ cup – 125 ml
⅓ cup – 80 ml

Grandpa's Breakfast Muffins

Ingredients:

3 cups breadcrumbs
2½ cups milk
1 tablespoon melted butter
2 teaspoons baking powder
½ teaspoon salt
1 cup flour
3 eggs, separated

Soak the breadcrumbs in the milk for 5 minutes. Then beat to a paste and add the egg yolks, salt, flour, baking powder and melted butter. Then fold in the beaten egg whites and bake in greased muffin pans in a moderate oven (350°F/180°C/gas mark 4) for 20 minutes. Delicious!

Amy's Chicken Pot Pie

Ingredients:

1.5 kg whole chicken
2 litres water
1 tsp salt
5 potatoes, diced
1 medium onion, diced
2 cups corn

For the dough:
2 cups of flour
½ tsp salt
2 eggs
4 tbsp water

Cook the chicken in 2 litres salted water until tender. Cool and debone, set aside. To the boiling broth add: potatoes, corn and onion. Cook for 10 minutes.

To prepare pot pie dough: combine flour and salt. Beat eggs with 4 tbsp water. With a fork work into the flour and salt until you have formed a stiff dough. Add more water if the mix is too dry. Roll the dough out on to a floured board until thin. Cut into 5 cm squares. Drop pot pie dough squares into boiling broth a few at a time and cook for about 20 minutes. Stir chicken pieces in and heat through.

Mom's Pecan Pie

Ingredients:

20 cm unbaked pie crust
1 cup light corn syrup
1 cup firmly packed dark brown sugar
3 eggs, slightly beaten
⅓ cup butter, melted
½ teaspoon salt
1 teaspoon vanilla
1 cup pecan halves

Heat oven to 350°F/180°C/gas mark 4. In a large bowl, combine corn syrup, sugar, eggs, butter, salt and vanilla; mix well. Pour filling into unbaked pie crust; sprinkle with pecan halves. Bake for 45 to 50 minutes or until centre is set. If crust or pie appears to be getting brown, cover with foil for the remaining baking time. Remove from oven and cool.

Heartland's Special Bran Mash

A bran mash is excellent for horses who have been exercising hard, or who are recovering from illness. This is my special recipe (for a horse of about 15.2 hh):

Fill a bucket half full of bran. Pour boiling water over it and stir until it becomes thoroughly wet (although not so wet that the bran flakes are swimming in water). Stir in a tablespoon of salt, two carrots (chopped into cubes or sticks, not circles), a tablespoon of honey and a handful of boiled barley or a handful of oats. Cover with a sack or cloth and leave until it is cool enough for the horse to eat.

Chapter Twelve

A Day in the Life of Heartland

6.30

Get up and grab one of Grandpa's homemade muffins and a mug of coffee if I have time – this depends on how much I've overslept!

7.00

Ty and Ben arrive and we feed the horses. Mom always used to say that it was better to keep horses on as simple a diet as possible, so we don't feed ready-made coarse mixes. For breakfast, the horses have bran, pony cubes, beet pulp and barley plus herbs if they need them. While the horses eat their grain, Ben, Ty and I take the haynets round to the stalls and refill the water buckets.

7.20

We start to muck out the stalls.

7.45

I usually get about two stalls done and then go in and take a shower and get ready for school.

8.00

I have some toast for breakfast (unless I'm too busy trying to finish my homework!) and then it's time to get the bus into school.

8.30

School (worse luck!). While I'm in school, Ben and Ty turn the horses out and finish cleaning out the stalls. After that, they sweep the yard and tidy the muckheap, then they start getting the horses in from the field. Each horse is groomed and then ridden or worked in hand (or sometimes just massaged and given lots of love and attention). For lunch, the horses have pony cubes and a slice of loose hay. Ben usually rides Red at lunchtime. After lunch, Ben and Ty continue to work the horses and fit in other jobs like refilling the feed-bins, restocking the small hay-store and cleaning tack.

3.30
I get back from school and get changed. Then I go out and work with the horses. Each horse at Heartland is assigned one main carer – either me, Ty or Ben. It seems to make the horses happier to have one special person to bond with. Being the main carer of a horse means that you are responsible for overseeing its progress and deciding on which training techniques or remedies are most suitable. Ben tends to have the bigger horses who are difficult to ride because he's tall (almost six foot) and he can stay on anything (he tells me it's superglue on the saddle that keeps him on!) Ty and I tend to split the nervous and abused horses between us. Ty is brilliant at helping horses who have physical injuries – Mom always used to say that he was born with healing hands. I love to work with horses who are scared or behaving badly – I like trying to figure out what's going on in their minds. Even though we all have our own special horses to work, we talk about all the horses and share ideas about how we can best help them.

So anyway, once I'm changed, I got out on to the yard and catch up on the day's news with Ty. After that I start grooming and working the horses that I'm in charge of. I normally have about three or four horses to work. I'll either ride them in the training ring or work them in the circular pen or sometimes they just need treating with T-Touch and aromatherapy oils. If there's time, Ty, Ben and I (and sometimes Lou and Soraya) will then go out for a trail ride to exercise the horses who are almost cured or the horses like Sundance and Jasmine who live at Heartland permanently.

5.00
We remove the droppings from the stalls and refill the water buckets. Then we bring in all the horses who need to be stabled at night (in the summer most of the ponies live out in the fields all the time). In the winter, we also have to rug the horses up for the night.

5.30
Suppertime (for the horses, not us!) For supper the horses have alfalfa, pony cubes, barley and cod liver oil (we always feed cod liver oil, it's great for keeping joints supple). In the winter, the older horses and horses who are in poor condition have a scoopful of warm boiled barley as well. All of the horses have a handful of cooked linseed jelly once a week. Linseed helps put a shine on horses' coats (but it has to be cooked – raw linseed is poisonous).

5.45
We give out the haynets and give the stalls a final check, then we sweep the feedroom and make up the feeds and haynets for the next morning.

6.15

Ben and Ty go home, although often Ty stays on to clean some tack with me. (There is *never* enough time to clean tack!)

7.00

I go inside and get showered and changed.

7.30

Grandpa, Lou and I eat supper – usually something Grandpa has cooked like a chicken casserole or baked ham.

8.30

I start my homework. (At least, this is what I'm supposed to do, but it doesn't always happen! Thank goodness for Matt and Soraya on the bus in the morning.)

11.00

I go to bed.

Chapter Thirteen

A Tour of Heartland

I thought I'd describe to you what Heartland's like as you walk round it so you can imagine it for yourself. To get to the farmhouse and the barns you turn off the main road out of Meadowville and walk up a long bumpy driveway. On either side of the driveway there are fields with dark-brown fencing. In the summer you'll see horses and ponies grazing in the sun, their tails swishing to keep away the flies. In each of the fields there are trees that provide shade. As you walk up the drive you'll see a small paddock on the right-hand side. It was Pegasus's paddock when he was alive. There are no horses in it now, just a young oak tree which marks his grave. I like to go and sit beside it sometimes and think about Pegasus and Mom.

At the top of the drive stands the old white weatherboarded farmhouse. Mom grew up here – and so did Grandpa. At the back is a small yard, a vegetable patch and a herb garden. We use the herbs to make remedies for the horses (and Grandpa uses some in his cooking!). Ty is in charge of looking after the herb garden. In the summer, he gathers herbs and either freezes or dries them so that we can use them throughout the winter when fresh herbs aren't available.

At right angles to the farmhouse is the front stable block. It's made out of old brick and has six stalls, each with a white door. The top half of each door is usually pinned back so the horses can look out. After Mom died we had a big tidy up of the yard and repainted all the stable doors and put up hanging baskets. Lou fills the baskets with pink and purple geraniums and they look really pretty – although she says they're a pain to water! I can see the front stable block from my bedroom and, in the summer, I love looking out and seeing the horses dozing as the sun sets.

If you go on up the yard with the stable block on your right, you pass the tackroom and rug store on your left. The rug store has trunks for keeping the winter rugs in during the summer months, and has a drying rack so that we can hang out muddy New Zealand rugs. The tackroom has saddle racks on the left-hand side and bridle hooks on the right. We have so much tack we hardly have room for it all! Some of the saddle racks have two saddles on them and in one corner there is a large wicker basket that is usually overflowing with boots and bandages. There is a floor-rug, it was once red but it is so faded and dusty now you can hardly tell what colour it was. There's a big pine cupboard at the far end for all the grooming kits. Above the trunk are hooks for our hard hats and for extra tack like martingales and lunging cavessons. To the right of the door is a shelf filled with Mom's books on alternative remedies and a white cupboard. We keep the first aid kit in there as well as all the aromatherapy oils and Bach Flower Remedies. The air in the tackroom smells of saddle soap and old leather. I love the tackroom, particularly in the winter when we come in to clean tack and we shut the door and put on a small portable heater. It's so cosy then – particularly if I've got a mug of Grandpa's hot chocolate – that I don't even mind cleaning tack!

Just past the tackroom on the right is the feed store. It is an old building with a grey flagstone floor, and there are loads of dusty cobwebs hanging from the beams inside. It doesn't matter how much you brush the floor, there always seem to be flakes of barley and wisps of hay caught in the cracks between the stones. Around

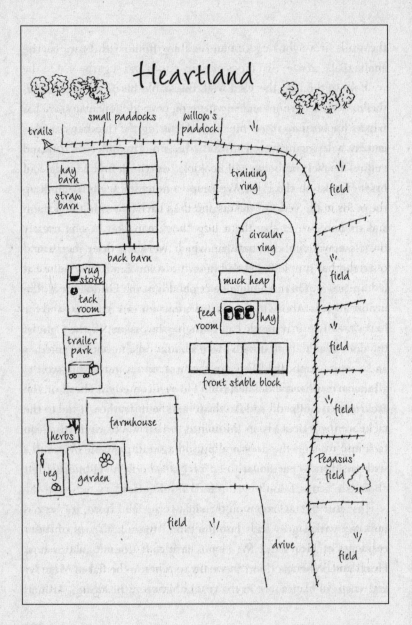

Heartland

trails

small paddocks

willow's paddock

hay barn

straw barn

back barn

training ring

circular ring

field

field

muck heap

rug store

tack room

feed room

hay

field

trailer park

front stable block

field

farmhouse

herbs

veg

garden

Pegasus' field

field

drive

field

the walls are eight huge metal feedbins filled with bran, barley, alfalfa, oats, maize, two types of pony cubes and sugarbeet. On the wall above the bins there's a whiteboard. We write down what all the horses are having to eat – what type of food, how many scoops, what supplements they need. In front of the feedbins there's usually a large dusty can of cod liver oil, two piles of battered yellow buckets, a bucket of soaking beet pulp and a couple of bran-encrusted sticks that we use for mixing the feeds. We mix up the feeds in the yellow buckets and then carry them to the horses' stalls where we empty them into their mangers. In one corner there's a wooden cupboard in which we keep dried herbs and other herbal supplements. Next to it is a small stove – we use it for heating water and boiling barley and linseed. Off the feedroom is a small haystore where we fill the haynets. We restock it every few days from the main hay barn. If the haynets aren't in the horses' stalls, they're usually lying in a muddle in one corner.

If you leave the feedstore and carry on up the yard, you pass the wheelbarrows and muckheap on your right. Straight ahead of you are the turn-out paddocks, to the left is the horses' barn and to the right are the training rings. Mom had the barn built eight years ago to house more horses. It has a big sliding door, twelve stalls and a wide aisle that runs down the centre. In the first stall on the left you'll see Sugarfoot, the little Shetland. If you carry on down the aisle you'll get to my pony Sundance's stall. Next to him is Jasmine. Sundance and Jasmine are two of the permanent residents at Heartland. We don't have many horses like that at Heartland. Whenever we can we try to rehome them, but Mom let me keep Sundance for my own and Jasmine is staying with us because she has bad windgalls – soft swellings above her fetlocks – that make her intermittently lame and not suitable for rehoming. She was a dressage pony before she came to Heartland and she is very sweet-natured. Not like Sundance. He's a real bully with other ponies!

If you leave the barn and walk past the turn-out paddocks on your left, then you get to the two sand training rings. There's a traditional rectangular ring with dressage markers, and a circular pen where we do join-up. Behind the paddocks and the rings is Teak's Hill – a wooded mountain with lots of brilliant trails to ride on. And that's about it – Heartland, my home.

My Favourite Non-Fiction Books

The Man Who Listens To Horses by Monty Roberts
Shy Boy by Monty Roberts
Considering the Horse by Mark Rashid
Horses Never Lie by Mark Rashid
Getting in Touch with Horses by Linda Tellington-Jones (with Sybil Taylor)
The Tellington T-Touch: A Holistic Approach to Training, Healing and Communicating with Animals by Linda Tellington-Jones (with Sybil Taylor)
A Modern Horse Herbal by Hilary Page Self
Plants, Potions and Oils for Horses by Chris Dyer
Bach Flower Remedies for Horses and Riders by Martin J. Scott (with Gael Mariani)
Imprint Training by Robert M. Miller
Centred Riding by Sally Swift

Don't miss Lauren Brooke's
exciting new horse series!

Chestnut Hill
The New Class

An extract...

Chapter One

"Dylan, we're almost there. Wake up, honey."

Dylan Walsh blinked her eyes open. Glancing out the window, she saw whitewashed fences lining lush green pastures. "What?" Dylan murmured. "Why'd you guys let me go to sleep?"

"We just got off the interstate a few minutes ago," her dad explained.

"You didn't miss anything." Dylan's mom looked over her shoulder into the backseat of the family SUV. "I thought you probably needed the rest."

Dylan rolled her eyes before she brushed her red hair behind her ears and turned her gaze back out the window. Dylan was relieved to know she'd soon be escaping her mother's overprotective ways. It was true that she hadn't been able to sleep a wink the night before. There had been too many things going through her head. She'd been looking forward to this day for so long – she was really on her way to Chestnut Hill! She searched the fields for any signs of horses, trying to gauge how close they were to the school. She wondered if all of Virginia was this picturesque.

Dylan followed the stretch of fence toward the horizon and her heart pounded when she saw the brick pillars that marked the entrance to the esteemed boarding school.

"This is it!" she yelled, recalling the first time she had visited the school. After the prospective-student weekend that spring, Dylan had been set on coming to Chestnut Hill.

She rolled down the window to get a better glimpse of the iron gates at the start of the drive. As her dad turned the car, Dylan's eyes focused on the Chestnut Hill crest. The chestnut tree (*what else?* she thought delightedly) with spreading roots and branches was worked into the ornate iron gate, along with the profile of a horse's head.

White rail fences continued on either side of the driveway, and Dylan shielded her eyes from the sun to scan the paddocks for the Chestnut Hill horses. She thought they were all beautiful, but she held her breath as she searched for one pony in particular.

Before she could find a familiar brown-and-white coat, the car turned to follow the gravel driveway, and the rest of the grounds came into view. Dylan leaned forward as they approached Old House, the magnificent white colonial building that had been the original school over one hundred years ago. With its tall white pillars, it gave Chestnut Hill a look of great Southern tradition. Now Old House just held faculty and administration offices, and the classrooms and science labs were in classic redbrick buildings on the other side of the campus. Ever since the fourth grade, when she read about it in *Horse and Rider* magazine, Dylan had wanted to attend Chestnut Hill for its top-tier riding programme. *I can't believe I'm actually here*, she thought, with a shiver of excitement. From the moment she had laid eyes on the campus that spring, she had been imagining this moment. Everything about the school was the best money could buy: the Olympic-size swimming pool, the indoor track, the art studio complete with ceramics workshop and kiln. And the school was known for high academic standards that prepared students for acceptance into the most competitive colleges, which pleased her parents.

Mr Walsh took a left turn, following the signs to the dorms on the north side of the campus. There were six houses, where students slept, studied, and generally hung out. Dylan already knew that she was in Adams House, which, very conveniently, was the dorm closest to the stable yard. She slid across the leather seat so she could look out the other window and tapped a drum roll with her fingers as they passed the wooden stables. *I'm going to be able to walk to the barn in less than five minutes*, she thought. *I'll be the most dedicated rider at Chestnut Hill. Just wait until team tryouts!*

Inside, a girl was carrying two buckets to the end stall. As the girl opened the door, Dylan caught sight of a magnificent black horse and twisted around so she could keep looking.

"Honey, you'll get whiplash if you keep turning your neck like that!" Mrs Walsh warned in a teasing tone.

Dylan straightened up, meeting her mother's eyes in the vanity mirror on the front passenger visor. "You need to brush your hair," Mrs Walsh told her. "It's flipping up again." She reached up to smooth her own neat red bob, but her tresses were already sleek and perfectly in place. Dylan might have inherited her mom's hair colour, but she sure didn't have the same patience to style and sculpt it.

"Maybe I'll just wear my hard hat." Dylan grimaced, running her fingers through her thick hair. "Then no one will notice." Her mom had been trying to persuade her to get a fringe, but she preferred having it all the same length, even if she needed a clip or a ponytail holder to keep it from falling into her eyes. "Hey, Dad, if you stop right now, I can get my hat out of the back."

Mr Walsh raised his eyebrows. "If we stop now, you'll disappear into the barn. Then you'd need a shower before you could pass your mom's inspection."

Dylan snapped her fingers. "You got me," she grinned. *Dad is so cool*, she thought, as she watched him pat her mom on the hand. *He totally gets me*. Her mom reached back and handed her a tortoiseshell hair clip. As Dylan reached for it, she switched off the DVD player built into the back of the front seat. She didn't mind not being able to watch the end of *Charlie's Angels*. Right now, real life was about one hundred times more exciting!

Dylan shifted to the middle of the backseat so she

could look out the front window. The road ahead was almost completely jammed with sports cars, SUVs, and luxury sedans. There didn't seem to be any parking spaces close to the dorm.

"Let's just stop here," Mr Walsh said, pulling over to the curb. "We can carry your luggage to the dorm."

Dylan had her hand on the door handle before her dad had even turned off the ignition. She jumped out onto the gravel path and took a deep breath. The air held a hint of autumn, but the sun, when it wasn't behind the clouds, was still at its summer strength. Everywhere Dylan looked, girls were getting out of cars, their arms full of garment bags and backpacks. Dylan followed her father around to the back of the SUV and pulled out the smaller of her two black suitcases. Mr Walsh let out a groan as he tested the weight of the larger bag.

"Come on, Dad. Here's your chance to prove what your country club membership does for you," Dylan said with a laugh. She doubted her dad had ever even been to the club's gym. He pretty much belonged for the golf and tennis, which he always ended up playing with his business partners. Without waiting to hear his reply, Dylan headed up the sidewalk in the direction of the dorms. She paused at the bottom of the sidewalk that led to the front door and tipped her head back to take in the white four-storey building. There were girls and parents on the steps leading up to the covered porch. Nobody had to wear the school uniform today, and everyone seemed to be taking advantage of that freedom. Like Dylan, lots of girls had on jeans and casual fitted tops, which was a relief. Dylan's mom had tried to get her to wear a pleated linen skirt with a cashmere tank, arguing that Dylan should try to make a good first impression.

The front porch cleared, and Dylan made her way up the steps and through the double doors. The foyer in Adams House seemed almost as busy as the unloading area outside and twice as noisy. Dylan caught her breath. In front of her, on either side of the room, was a formal double staircase that swept upward in a swoosh of crimson carpet. At the top of the stairs, a Chinese-style vase with a colourful and elaborate arrangement of flowers sat on a polished antique table. Sunlight streamed in through a beautiful stained-glass window on the second floor, making Dylan squint. *I feel like I'm in* Gone with the Wind, she thought. She hovered uncertainly, not having a clue where she should go.

"Excuse me!" An older student carrying a cello case stopped right in front of her.

"Oh, sorry," Dylan said, embarrassed, realizing she was blocking the door. She stepped to one side and placed her suitcase on the waxed hardwood floor. *Way to go, Walsh. No better way to look like a first-year student than standing right in the doorway with a dumb look on your face.* She took a deep breath and noticed a lovely scent of jasmine in the air. She tracked the aroma to another arrangement of flowers, this one in a cut glass vase on a polished maple table, the top of which was dappled with light. Dylan glanced up to see a magnificent chandelier hanging above her, dripping with crystals. She couldn't believe this was campus housing. It looked more like an interior design showcase.

"Dylan Walsh?" A smiling woman with dark curly hair appeared beside her. She glanced down at a clipboard and then back at Dylan. "Welcome to Adams House. Don't worry," she said. "This is the only day of the year when all chaos breaking loose is officially allowed." She held out her hand. "I'm Mrs Herson, your housemother. If you have any problems settling in, come see me and I'll try my best to help." Mrs Herson's brown eyes twinkled as she handed Dylan a map. "Noel Cousins, our dorm prefect, will show you where your room is, if you're ready."

"That would be great," Dylan said, reaching down for her suitcase.

Mrs Herson waved to a tall girl with wavy auburn hair who was just coming down the staircase. "Noel," she called. "This is Dylan Walsh. Can you take her up to Room Two?"

"Sure," the senior nodded, walking over.

"Noel is co-captain of the senior jumping team," Mrs Herson told Dylan. "So you already have something in common."

"Co-captain? That's great!" Dylan said, standing up a little straighter as she made eye contact with the senior. "I mean, isn't that what everyone wants? If they're in the riding programme, I mean." She winced. *What was going on?* Dylan was used to being so composed and knowing just what to say, but her words sounded all jumbled.

Noel smiled at the compliment. "I'd like to say it's not a big deal, but…"

"You don't want to lie, right?" Dylan relaxed enough to grin at the senior. She looked around for her parents, and, spotting them in the middle of the foyer, she waved for them to come over.

The Walshes followed Noel up the scarlet-carpeted staircase. Halfway up, the prefect paused and pointed down at a pair of doors leading off the foyer. "Before I forget, the seventh-grade common room and study hall are through there," she told Dylan. "I'm sure you'll log plenty of hours in those rooms."

As Dylan leaned forward to look down the corridor, a girl with her hair in cornrows started down the stairs, waving to someone below. She accidentally bumped against Dylan as she tried to get past. "Hey, watch it, Tanisha," Noel warned and gave Dylan an apologetic smile. "Typical upperclassman attitude. They forget they were rookies once, too!"

"I heard that," Tanisha called over her shoulder.

Listening to their banter Dylan bit her lip. Right now, it was hard to imagine she'd ever feel that comfortable around this place. It wasn't like her to be overwhelmed. She vaguely remembered her first day of kindergarten, and even then, she'd had a very practical, can-do attitude about taking on new things.

At the top of the stairs Noel turned left and walked down a hallway to a second, narrower flight of stairs.

"Your dorm room is up here," she explained. "You know, I started off in Room Two. I've always thought it's kind of lucky. Every year that I've been here, a first-year student from Room Two has made it onto the equestrian team."

"That's good news. I'm hoping to try out for the team," Dylan admitted, her heart beating faster.

"Yeah?" Noel glanced at her. "Competition's going to be tough this year, then. I know that Lynsey Harrison, who's rooming with you, is trying out, too." She paused to wait for Dylan's parents, who were looking rather out of breath. "Everyone gets used to all of the stairs after a while! There is a rickety elevator in the back, but Mrs Herson gives us a lecture on the importance of exercise if she catches us using it."

Noel held open the heavy fire doors at the top of the stairs, then led the way down a broad hall, past open doors where Dylan caught glimpses of girls unpacking. Her stomach flipped again as Noel stopped. This was it! Her room at Chestnut Hill!

"Welcome to Adams Room Two," Noel declared, opening the door. "You're rooming with Felicity Harper and Lynsey Harrison. You have a couple of hours to unpack and have a look around and then, at five o'clock, the school will be meeting in the chapel for our first convocation of the year." Noel stepped aside to allow Dylan to enter. "If you need anything, you can head down to Room Five. We're all seniors. We're a little more sane than the underclassmen. They'll calm down, though. It's just because it's the first day."

"Oh, it's OK," Dylan said. "I can handle a little insanity now and then."

"That's good to hear." A dimple flashed in Noel's cheek as she gave Dylan's parents a courteous smile. "Later," she said with a wave before slipping from the room.

Dylan let out a sigh. She hoped she had made a good impression.

Her mother stepped past her, hanging Dylan's garment bag over a chair. "Oh, this is lovely! Your lilac bedsheets will look fabulous against those floral drapes." She went over to feel the material. "You really lucked out."

Dylan followed her mom and looked around. There were three twin beds in the room, each with a matching cedar wardrobe and dresser with a pull-out desk top. The wood was the colour of warm honey, glowing in the sunlight that poured through the window at the far end of the room. It appeared that the bed immediately underneath the window had already been taken. Four cognac-coloured leather suitcases with the initials *LAH* were stacked next to it, and the bed itself was covered with shoe boxes and garment bags. Dylan set her own suitcase just inside the door.

Dylan's dad heaved the other bag over the threshold and straightened up, rubbing his back. "And I thought *you* packed too much. I pity whoever carried *her* luggage up those stairs," he joked, nodding toward the pile of bags by the window.

"That's right, Dad!" Dylan responded. "You should

never take me for granted. See what an easygoing daughter I am?"

"Yes, an easygoing daughter who begged incessantly for three years to go away to boarding school," her dad replied in a slightly accusatory tone.

Dylan knew that her father had wanted her to stay at home. She was an only child, and her dad had always treated her as though she were a friend as much as a daughter. They would swap jokes at dinner, go fishing on weekends, and, once in a while, go trail riding together. Dylan thought it was ironic – her dad had given her his love of horses, and that love had made her want to attend a boarding school over four hundred miles from home.

She walked to the far end of the room and leaned her elbows on the windowsill. The view looked straight across campus, but more importantly, it had a great view of the stable yard, where she could see a beautiful bay gelding being led in from the field.

"Look at the lines on that Thoroughbred. I bet he can really jump, huh?" Dylan's dad said as he joined her at the window. "I guess we would take him at Riverlea."

Dylan and her dad liked to daydream that they would buy a ranch out West and name it Riverlea. They'd have a dozen ponies and horses and then some cattle. Dylan knew it would never happen – for starters, she was more focused on equitation and jumping than riding Western and driving cattle – but it was fun to talk about. They sometimes did it just to tease Dylan's mom, who would consider moving to a ranch only if she could fly her hair stylist out weekly and get Prada home-delivered.

Mr Walsh pointed to a snazzy chestnut backing out of a trailer.

Dylan felt her stomach flip with excitement as she watched the everyday commotion of the stable: buckets, haynets, lead ropes, travelling wraps, horses, horses, horses! *Get me down there!* She couldn't wait to start pitching in. She'd spent most of the summer hanging out with her friends at the local stables, riding every day. Her instructor had let her try different mounts all summer, so it had felt as if she had half a dozen gorgeous ponies of her own. But the last few days had been filled with packing and sorting out her bedroom at home, so Dylan was anxious to get into the saddle again.

"Look at this set!" Mrs Walsh exclaimed, eyeing the suitcases on Dylan's roommate's bed and running her fingers over the largest one. "I'm sure I saw one just like it in Takashimaya on Fifth Avenue."

"They must belong to Lynsey Harrison," Dylan told her.

Mrs Walsh straightened up, beaming. "The Harrisons! Of course! I knew I'd heard the name. There was an article in *Vanity Fair* last month that mentioned Mrs Harrison's last fundraising event. The banquet was held at their home, and it was such a beautiful house. I'm sure Lynsey will make a wonderful friend for you, Dylan."

"Mom! Like I'd choose her as a friend because her

family has enough money to be featured in *Vanity Fair*!" Dylan said. *Why does mom always get so hung up on America's A-List?* She frowned.

Her dad held up his hands in a peacemaking gesture. "Whoa, I'm sure that's not what your mom meant. After all, any of the girls here are going to come from..." He looked left then right and dropped his voice to a whisper, "...moneyed backgrounds."

Dylan grinned and threw a pillow at him from the selection on the bed closest to her.

"Is that the bed you want, honey?" Mrs Walsh asked. "We'll help you unpack."

"Um, it's OK, Mom. I think I can handle it. Anyway, I thought I'd wait until Felicity arrives so we can see who wants which bed." *In other words, I'm ready for you to leave so I can go check out the horses*, she translated silently, catching her father's eye.

"Come on, hon. I'm sure Dylan can handle it. If we linger too long, she might actually think about how much she'll miss us. We don't want her to do that."

"Dad!" Dylan didn't want them to think she didn't want them around at all, but her urge to explore was too strong to suppress.

He caught her up in a huge hug, planting a kiss on the top of her head. "You have your cell phone, so be sure to call us if you need anything," he told her. "And even if you don't."

"Sure thing," Dylan replied, her voice muffled as she pressed her head into her father's shoulder.

She hugged her mom next and, as Dylan inhaled the

familiar Amouage perfume, a wave of homesickness gripped her. *This is going to be tougher than I thought.* It was going to be so weird being away from home for this long; this was way different from summer camp, where it was for just a few weeks, or from visiting her grandparents' house in the country. "Call us later," Mrs Walsh told her, reaching out to tuck a strand of hair behind Dylan's ear. "And don't forget your Aunt Ali is here for you."

"Yeah, right. Me and two hundred other girls," Dylan pointed out, but she smiled to show she was joking. Dylan hadn't known what to think when she had first heard that her aunt had taken over as Director of Riding at Chestnut Hill. Dylan's parents had already signed all her admittance paperwork, so it had been too late for her to change her mind. Dylan had always loved visiting Ali's stables in Kentucky, but this was different. She couldn't help but think that it would be awkward living on the same campus and having Ali as her riding instructor. *So much for my new independence!* Plus, Dylan didn't want the other girls thinking that she was going to get any favoritism from Ali. She wanted to make it at Chestnut Hill on her own. But right now, Dylan had to admit that the thought of a familiar face was sort of comforting. *Great. I'll be wanting a pacifier next.*

"I'll call later," she promised her parents. "Or you can call me when you get home." She walked to the door and watched them all the way down to the end of the hall. They turned and waved before disappearing through the double doors, and Dylan went back into the room. Suddenly it felt very empty. She sat down on the edge of the bed as a funny sensation, kind of like the butterflies she felt before a riding competition, hit her stomach. *Get a grip*, she told herself. *I'm at the best school in Virginia, which has an incredible riding programme, and my favorite pony in the whole world is waiting for me down in the stable.* She lay back on the bed and closed her eyes. She had a framed photo of Morello, the paint gelding, in her backpack, but she could picture him just as clearly in her head.

She'd first met him that summer when she'd spent a couple of weeks on her aunt's farm in Kentucky. Dylan smiled as she thought back to how quickly she'd become smitten with the pony. He had the cutest personality ever! He was adventurous and mischievous – Ali had said that Dylan and Morello had a lot in common. The first time Dylan had seen him, Morello had been loose in the stables, snuffling at the feed room door. Ali had quickly caught him and put him back in his stall, playfully reprimanding the pony as she slid home the bottom bolt. Morello could undo the top lock with his teeth, Ali explained. Then she told the story about the time he wandered up to the farmhouse and was caught pushing his way through the kitchen screen door.

Morello could be a challenge in the stable, but he was a dream in the ring. He had a great rhythmic pace, and his jumps exploded with energy. Dylan had never known a pony that made riding such fun.

And, while Dylan didn't want to flatter herself, she thought Morello had been just as taken with her. By the end of her stay, he would whinny whenever he saw her and come to her at the paddock gate.

Dylan's apprehension about Ali being accepted as the riding director quickly dissolved when she heard that Morello would make the move, too. Of course! He would be perfect for Chestnut Hill. And so would Ali. Her mom had made a big point about how this job was a great opportunity for Ali – a fresh start. Dylan knew her aunt was a talented instructor. Her students had dominated at the show they went to when Dylan was visiting.

Dylan thought about the photo of Morello in her bag. It had been taken at the Lexington Horse Show, where they had placed third in the Turnout class. Dylan had wanted to compete in a jumping class, but her mom insisted Ali would be busy enough with her regular students. Still, when Dylan claimed the yellow rosette, Mrs Walsh had acted like she'd won a ribbon at a major competition – and on reflection, Dylan thought she'd done pretty well to get Morello's white patches as clean as she had, and her braids were always neat and tight. Not all judges would rank a paint that high against all the stylish ponies at an A-level show.

Dylan looked up at the sound of the door opening. She felt her heart jolt as she prepared herself for the fact that her parents had probably come back for more good-byes. Instead, it was Noel Cousins who smiled in at her before stepping back to let a petite girl with shoulder-length blond hair enter the room.

Dylan stood up and helped the girl drag in her suitcases. "Welcome to Room Two!" she said, feeling like a veteran. Acting confident seemed to ease the butterfly battle in her stomach.

"Thanks." The girl smiled, pulling her hair back from her cute, heart-shaped face.

"Dylan, this is Felicity," Noel said. "I thought you could show her around. Just make sure you're both at the convocation."

"No problem." Dylan waited for Noel to shut the door behind her before turning to her new roommate. "How are you doing, Felicity?"

"I haven't been called that in ages," the girl replied, almost in a whisper. "It sounds so formal. You can just call me Honey."

Dylan blinked when she heard her new roommate's polished accent, but she didn't miss a beat. "Nice to meet you, Honey. I'm Dylan. I'm from Connecticut."

"Oh, I'm from … well, I used to live in London, in England. We've only just moved out here – my father is a professor at the University of Virginia," Honey explained. She nodded toward the suitcases on the far bed. "Are they yours?"

"No!" Dylan said quickly. "They belong to Lynsey Harrison. I like to think of her as BBB."

Honey turned and raised a thin blond eyebrow.

"Best Bed Bagger," Dylan translated, her face

perfectly straight. "I mean, I guess it's first come, first served, so I don't really blame her."

Honey smiled. "So we get to choose between the other two, then?"

"You go first, I'm cool with either one."

"Well, if you're sure you don't mind, I'll take this one." Honey pointed to the bed nearest the door. She skirted Dylan's bed and lifted up a stylish plaid backpack. She unzipped the front pocket and pulled out a stack of photographs.

"Hey, he's gorgeous!" Dylan exclaimed, spotting a picture of a showy chestnut pony jumping over parallel bars. "Is he yours?"

"He was," Honey confirmed with a wistful sigh. "His name's Rocky. My parents bought him for me when I was nine, but I had to leave him in England." Honey reached out to trace her finger across the glass in the photo frame.

"That must have been really hard," Dylan said sympathetically. She had never had a pony of her own, but she knew how difficult it had been saying goodbye to Morello after riding him for only two weeks.

She figured it would be kind of rude to head straight for the stable yard now that Honey had arrived. She started to unpack, almost wishing she had taken her parents' offer to help as she realized just how much she had brought with her – her school uniform, riding stuff, clothes for wearing around the dorm, clothes for formal dinners, not to mention books and photos. And at the bottom of the case, there was a stuffed panda bear named Pudding that her grandmother had knitted when Dylan was a baby. He was a bit squashed after being stuffed in the oversized suitcase, but she gave him a shake, pummeled his nose back into shape, and propped him on her pillow.

Honey glanced over and caught her eye. For a moment Dylan paused. *Is it totally babyish bringing a stuffed bear to boarding school?* But then Honey wordlessly took out a small brown bear and tucked him under the top of her duvet, before flashing a grin at Dylan.

"There was no way I was coming here without Woozle!" she joked.

Relaxing, Dylan unwrapped the layer of tissue paper from around the first photograph. It showed her dad holding up a sign for his engineering company's new branch, with his other arm around Dylan's mom. The next photo was one of Dylan standing next to Morello, the yellow ribbon clipped to his bridle.

"Oh, do you ride, too?" Honey asked, leaning over to look. "What a fabulous pony!"

"This is Morello. He's actually here at Chestnut Hill. He's a little spoiled. He'll probably expect a bunch of organic carrots off a silver platter when he sees me," Dylan told her. "I was about to go down to the stable before you got here. Do you want to head down together?" She glanced at her watch. "We've got lots of time before convocation."

Honey's brown eyes lit up. "That sounds good."

Dylan grinned, figuring things couldn't get much better – and she'd only been at Chestnut Hill for an hour. She sprang to her feet. "Let's go!"